CODE NAME JOSHUA

CODE NAME JOSHUA

S. K. ALFSTAD

TATE PUBLISHING
AND ENTERPRISES, LLC

Published by Tate Publishing & Enterprises, LLC
127 E. Trade Center Terrace | Mustang, Oklahoma 73064 USA
1.888.361.9473 | www.tatepublishing.com

Tate Publishing is committed to excellence in the publishing industry. The company reflects the philosophy established by the founders, based on Psalm 68:11,
"The Lord gave the word and great was the company of those who published it."

Book design copyright © 2012 by Tate Publishing, LLC. All rights reserved.
Cover design by Joel Uber
Interior design by Mary Jean Archival

Published in the United States of America

ISBN: 978-1-62295-006-5
1. Fiction / Christian / Suspense
2. Fiction / War & Military
12.11.12

PART ONE

PASSING THE MANTLE

Chapter 1

NIGHTMARES

Dull, gloomy, and drizzling—a fall night in Sarajevo; cold, wet—wanting to go home. End of shift; almost done. People walking briskly, shoulders slumped, heads bowed, hands in pockets. Children huddled close to parent, feeling safe… Car driving slower than usual. Window rolls down. Something bad is about to happen. Raising my M4, raising my assault rifle, still raising my weapon—slow motion. I can't move any faster—almost paralyzed. Through the haze, the unmistakable sight of a gun barrel comes out of the partially opened car window. The eerie ring of submachine gun fire is echoing off the buildings. Glass shatters. Chaotic screams. Like a phantom, the car is gone. The soft, innocent, gentle, beautiful, scared eyes of a little girl—

Magnus woke up startled. How long will this dream, and memory, of that fatal night haunt him? How long will the guilt stay with him? Magnus turned his head toward his wife. He lightly stroked her cheek with the back of his fingers, and gently brushed back her hair with his fingertips. A few minutes later, he drifted back to sleep.

Dark—Audra in the distance. Trying to reach her. Running… Running… Tired, stiff, and feeling helpless—I must save her. For the first time, real, almost paralyzing fear that I can't. The truth is I can't. She falls to the ground—dead. When I finally get to her, the lifeless, open eyes of the love of my life are peering at me.

Robert stared at the ceiling—numb. The thought didn't startle him anymore. For once in his life, that deep down confidence and assurance that somehow, some way, no matter how grim the situation looked, he could figure a way out, was shaken. Staring at the ceiling, he came to the conclusion that he was too old; he was way past his prime. What was tormenting him the worst was the thought that he should have reached this conclusion before that last mission.

0730 hours, 05 March 2007, Central Intelligence Agency headquarters, Langley, Virginia:

They've never met. As usual, Robert is ten minutes early, dressed in a smart, dark-blue business suit and maroon tie. The black high-end running shoes and sophisticated sports watch were the only things slightly out of sorts with his attire, but it looked good. As usual, Magnus was a few minutes late, wearing jeans, t-shirt, dress jacket, and desert Army boots, appearing slightly uninterested. The director's office was very stark but modern. Both men waited for the invitation to sit down.

"Gentlemen, please have a seat. Robert Steele—Magnus Stone. Robert, we feel Magnus has the potential to be an excellent agent for us, and we want him to be mentored by the best: you."

"I'm flattered," said Robert, "but why do we need a new agent?"

"Pardon me," interrupted Magnus, "but I don't recall applying for the job."

"Pardon me, Mr. Stone, I wasn't finished with the director," Robert said, peering at Magnus.

Magnus glared back at Robert, on the verge of making a witty, seething comeback, but out of respect, he acquiesced.

"Excuse me Mr. Steele."

Deep down, Robert was impressed with how Magnus handled that; however, it did nothing to ease the tension in the office.

Without missing a beat, and not at all bothered, the director began to answer Robert's question.

"You and I have always been indelibly forthright with each other, no need to change now," Robert agreed.

As the director continued, he became visibly nervous.

"Well, I don't want to start out with the polite, customary platitudes to set you up for the hard news. Robert, you're almost

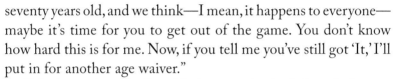

seventy years old, and we think—I mean, it happens to everyone—maybe it's time for you to get out of the game. You don't know how hard this is for me. Now, if you tell me you've still got 'It,' I'll put in for another age waiver."

"Maybe you're right," said Robert in a hushed, dignified voice, which is not at all what the director expected.

During this whole conversation, Magnus looked intently at Robert, occasionally glancing at the director, his foot crossed over his knee, and his elbow resting on the arm of the chair, with his fist resting against his mouth. There was a lengthy stretch of silence.

"May I ask what all this has to do with me," inquired Magnus.

"Everything, young man; I want you to be the next 'Joshua,'" responded the director.

"Which means what?"

The director straightened himself and stated, "Incredible honor, dignity, and the awesome responsibility to protect the world from those who wish to rule it. However, these people don't have creditable intentions, but rather, self-serving, destructive ones."

"Uh, with all due respect, Sir, I think you have my resume mixed up with someone else," replied Magnus.

The director began to brief the summary in front of him: "1995 to 2004: Enlisted in the United States Army. Because of outstanding service, you were encouraged to go to Ranger School. You successfully became a member of that elite force and performed admirably in that capacity. It was duly noted that during your time in this intense, demanding program, you also took care of your blind grandmother, and only known guardian, at the time while supplementing your sister's college tuition, working, against the rules I might add, on the side to support them. With the program's tight scrutiny, I still don't know how you pulled that one off."

"To be honest, Sir, 'working' is an interpretational stretch. Let's just say I 'earned money,' and I did get caught."

The director lightened up at that moment when Magnus was up front about his transgression; however, Robert maintained a serious demeanor.

The director continued, "In 2003, as a Sergeant First Class in the Army, you received a Bronze Star in Operation Iraqi Freedom I. In 2004, you were invited to train for the Green Berets." At this, Magnus became noticeably uncomfortable. "Magnus," continued the director after a brief pause. "After a very comprehensive investigation, we consider you exonerated of the crime you committed in the Army. I certainly don't condone what you did. However, given the surrounding circumstances, I can give you a clean slate. I know you are truly remorseful." Magnus stared away, not convinced.

"Now, as for you Robert," started the director. "After Magnus finishes JOT, I want you two to work on the Muslov Deshnue case together. I want your expertise and experience to begin to be imparted to Magnus. While Magnus is in training, you, me, and the rest of the team will coordinate all the intel we have received thus far."

Robert, while looking at Magnus, responded, "He's known for his innovative genius in computer programs that could potentially probe the human mind. He's also reclusive."

The director added, "Yes, well, I believe he's removed the word 'potential;' he has succeeded, and his intentions are extremely questionable."

"Which are?" questioned Magnus.

"I believe trying to instigate World War III, most likely. And then, because of his mastery of this new computer technology, be in a position to be a very powerful, influential man in the post-war future."

"I must admit," said Robert, "I'm not comfortable with this idea. No offense to the young, Mr. Stone, but I know there are more qualified and experienced agents in the UTD for such an urgent mission. Besides, he hasn't even started JOT."

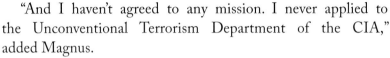

"And I haven't agreed to any mission. I never applied to the Unconventional Terrorism Department of the CIA," added Magnus.

With a confident, sly grin, the director stated, "No one applies to the UTD; people are selected—very few."

"Yes, well, I know it's an honor, but I'm not sure I want to be 'selected,'" said Magnus.

At this, Robert was visibly irritated. He gently, but firmly scolded Magnus. "I realize you're relatively young, but that's no excuse for your lack of appreciation."

With that, Magnus stood up, nodded his head, and started for the door saying, "I have another engagement. Excuse me gentlemen."

"Good riddance," Robert said.

A snicker came from Magnus as he walked out.

The director chased him down. "Magnus, I have something I want to show you," pleaded the director as he pulled out his wallet and showed him a worn-out, aged picture. "The man on the left is Russell J. Stone, your dad, one of the finest men I ever served with, and a good, good friend."

Magnus's eyes glistened with moisture as he looked at the photograph. He quickly composed himself and said, "You mean the man that left his family a little over twenty years ago. I'm glad he was your good friend, but that means nothing to me."

"Magnus," continued the director, "There were a lot of overwhelming circumstances surrounding his need to leave and go into hiding. He did it for your family's safety. It broke his heart—believe me." Magnus listened intently. "Robert knew your dad also. He knows you're his son. I'm going to talk to him some more, and I want you to take a few days to think about this assignment. Above all, pray."

"Pray?" questioned Magnus as he dropped his head and slightly furrowed his brow.

"Yes young man—pray."

CHAPTER 2

THE CALL

Lazo, Siberia, 13 October 2001:
In an unassuming building in the warehouse district, a light shined through a cloudy, dirty window. Inside, the figure of a man was slumped over a computer keyboard. It was hard to tell which monitor he was looking at because there were three in front of him. Various junk food wrappers and soda cans were scattered around him, on the floor, on the monitors, and on what table space there was.

⟶➤◆⟵

Muslov Deshnue was born in Bucharest, Romania in 1959 to a prominent family. At an early age, he was a certified genius. All of his teachers commented that they had never encountered anyone who had ever come close to matching his intelligence. Despite his mental gifts, he acted like a normal boy. He interacted well with his classmates, and he was a good son. He grew up in a solid, loving family. His dad was a well-respected journalist. His mother was a content housewife. His two older sisters and younger brother worked hard in school and excelled. They lived in a spacious, four bedroom home, with a large yard and a beautiful garden. The children, along with the whimsical black lab, played often and happily in the back yard.

In 1976, all of his family tearfully, but proudly, said good-bye to the young man Muslov at the train station as he started his journey through academic excellence, starting at Oxford where he received a scholarship. He started out studying science, which he truly loved. However, for a while this took a back seat to his new love, a relatively novel thing called computer programming.

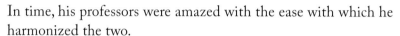

In time, his professors were amazed with the ease with which he harmonized the two.

The Ceausescu reign started to be exposed. This communist dictatorship flourished as the Romanian people struggled. The media, fed-up and fearless, began to increase the criticism of Nikolai Ceausescu. Some outspoken detractors of the regime mysteriously disappeared or were killed. Everyone knew why. However, the momentum for reform was so strong that force and intimidation could not stop it. The government would come to a disgraceful end in 1989.

Boris Deshnue was one of the journalists who would not be intimidated. He refused to be silent. His conviction that the regime was evil drove him. He gained a lot of attention; especially from Ceausescu. This was the beginning of the end for Boris.

Mrs. Deshnue was growing concerned when her husband hadn't come home from work at 1940 hours on that wicked night. She called his office, friends, and then the police—with much distrust. Her misgivings were founded. For it was the police that "arrested" Mr. Deshnue late in the afternoon. However, they didn't take him to the police station. His body was found the next day in an alleyway. The perpetrators wanted his corpse to be discovered. They wanted him to be an example. They demanded people know what happens to outspoken critics.

At 1046 hours, 28 February 1979, while Muslov diligently sat in his quantum physics class; a distressed woman quietly entered the classroom and tapped Muslov on the shoulder. She motioned for him to follow her. When they were in the hall, she said in a voice that couldn't hide her anxiety, "You have a phone call in my office."

That phone call would forever change Muslov and possibly the world. After he hung up, Muslov showed absolutely no emotion. He walked out of the office, oblivious to the pats on the shoulder, and the offers of comfort and a listening ear. He quietly walked back to class and resumed his note taking. The staff was concerned by his stone face. Later, in his room, he methodically packed. He was oblivious and unresponsive to his roommates' gestures of consolation. His friends, too, were concerned. Muslov was a brick wall. On the train ride home, he didn't look left or right, only straight ahead. He was the same emotionless stone rampart at the funeral, with his mother and siblings, and when he returned to school. Everyone knew something wasn't right with the young genius. He never changed his expression throughout his college career. He graduated with the highest honors. Some around him feared him. They sensed he was a time bomb.

CHAPTER 3

THE AGREEMENT

After flying to Austin, Texas, Robert knocked on the door at 1240 Oak. It was a nice, modest condominium. The neighborhood was clean and middle class. A beautiful young woman answered the door with an equally beautiful baby girl in her arms.

"Good evening. I'm Robert Steele here to meet with Magnus," he politely said.

With a sweet smile, Andrea replied, "Please come in." As Robert walked by the two, he gently touched the cheek of little Dawn. She shyly smiled and buried her little head in her mother's shoulder.

In a respectful but distant manner, Magnus shook Robert's hand and invited him to have a seat. They sat comfortably in one another's presence. There was a bond already forming between the two, though neither wanted to reveal the mutual admiration and respect for the other.

Robert started, "I take it this is your lovely family."

"It is," responded Magnus, with a wry smile, "You should try the marriage and family thing. It's good."

Robert shifted in his chair and, for a split second, looked uncomfortable. Robert's reputation preceded him. He was a ladies' man. Besides being one of the most athletic, crafty, and smartest agents, he was also handsome and confident with women.

Robert started, "Well, yes, let's get to business shall we?" Magnus couldn't contain a grin.

"Young man," Robert continued, "I've been studying this case concerning Muslov Deshnue. This man could be the most dangerous I've encountered yet. He's a new breed of maniacal villain. The word 'new' concerns me. I don't think I've ever been this apprehensive about a case. I have to humble myself. I'm getting old. I'm not as sharp as I use to be. This is hard for me to admit, but I have to do it… We need each other, young man."

Robert had a hunch that Magnus was dealing with his own doubts and fears. That night in Sarajevo still haunted Magnus. The thought that he could have, should have, reacted quicker was ever-present like an unwanted neighbor. The thought that maybe he'd lost his edge continually lingered on top of the shame he felt about being an *ex con*.

"Why me?" questioned Magnus.

"You've got the moxie and inherited traits from your dad."

With obvious irritation in his voice, Magnus snapped, "You and the director keep bringing up my old man. You keep talking about his 'qualities.' The only quality I remember is the absent father. It's almost dinner time for my family and me." Standing up, Magnus continued, "If you'll excuse us. Good evening, Mr. Steele."

Before Robert reached the door, he stopped, turned, and handed Magnus a manila envelope marked, *Confidential*. Since Robert arrived, Magnus was curious about the packet.

Robert said, "I'm requesting a gentleman's agreement between us. Read this dossier. Read it carefully. Study it, okay?" With this last word, Robert extended his hand. Magnus looked at the extremity for what seemed like an awkwardly long time. Finally, he shook it and took the envelope. Robert trusted the handshake. The integrity of Magnus's dad and his son were above reproach.

CHAPTER 4

THE FAMILY MAN

Andrea knew not to force it. When Magnus was ready to talk and share, he would. Not until then. She knew he would eventually; he almost always did. However, this time was taking longer than usual. While Dawn was curled up, asleep in Daddy's lap, Magnus thoroughly scrubbed the dossier. He went over it with a highlighter and a pen; Magnus was thorough that way. He wasn't necessarily committed to taking on the mission, but he wanted to make sure his questions were well thought out for the director and Robert. There were too many new and unknown facets to this mission and to Muslov Deshnue. *Traveling via a computer program into someone's mind and subconscious?* Apparently Deshnue wasn't a skilled leader. He wasn't adept at rallying people to follow him. He had no history in being trained militarily.

Lying in bed, looking at the ceiling, Magnus spoke, "What's your opinion on this mission?" He knew Andrea had a "sense" of what was happening. She is very perceptive.

She responded, "Is it possible that Dawn and I will lose you?" She laid her head on his chest, then she continued, "If you don't take it, could we lose more?"

"Incredible," Magnus said. "How did you know this had such importance?"

"Mr. Steele doesn't work on insignificant missions," she responded.

Magnus was surprised, "How do you know about Robert Steele?"

Calmly, Andrea said, "I could tell by his presence—his demeanor."

"You're right," Magnus said. "I suppose you can read the dossier. If it were top secret, Mr. Steele wouldn't have presented it the way he did. There aren't any details per se. This guy named Muslov Deshnue, a Romanian, is a wacked out genius. Supposedly he can influence people by tapping into their subconscious."

"That's enough. We need to pray about it. You need to pray about it."

"You have the stronger connection to the Divine. That's your department."

"I won't push it, but it's almost time for Dawn to see her Daddy assume the role of spiritual leader of the home."

Magnus, a bit frustrated, got up and went to the bathroom. Andrea didn't care. She believed strongly that it needed to be said. Deep down, Magnus knew it too. He's been living on the prayers of his grandmother and wife.

———⟶●⟵———

Magnus's grandmother, Dorcus, raised him after his mother's break down. Magnus's dad was one of the most accomplished agents in the CIA. As a young boy, the only thing Magnus knew about him was that he was gone a lot. When he was home, he tried to be a good father. He went through the motions. Magnus's dad played football in the backyard with the kids, helped them with their homework, and tucked Magnus and his brother and sister into bed, but Russell Stone was always tired and distant when he did it, almost like a robot. He tried, but the heart wasn't there. When Magnus's dad left for work, he'd be gone for days, weeks, and sometimes months. His mother would cry for too long, from Magnus's perspective, and she slipped into a deep depression. Where Russell went, no one really knew. He had to go to some 'mysterious work.' The secrets literally killed the mother and tore the family apart—almost. Magnus's loving, godly grandmother stepped in, raised, and saved, Magnus and his older brother and younger sister.

Magnus and his brother grew apart. David defended and idolized his father. Magnus thought David was ridiculous and his dad was a lousy parent. Francesca was confused. She was too young to understand.

Magnus assumed, and performed brilliantly, the role of protective brother. Once, when an elementary classmate of Francesca's was bullying her, she cried and finally confided in Magnus. He went to the girl's home. He tried to politely tell her father about the situation and asked him to correct it. The man didn't care and was irritated for the waste of his time. Magnus called him outside and told him they would have to then settle this via brawl. While the thirty-five year old man walked toward Magnus, he laughed at the bravery of the sixteen year old. About a minute later, the man wasn't laughing, and his daughter never terrorized Francesca again.

Although suffering from failing eye sight, Dorcus never let it get down her faith. She was a gentle, strong, hopeful and loving woman. Magnus was confused that such a wonderful person could have such a worthless son. This bitterness that Magnus had in his heart toward his dad, while having some positive effects, mostly hindered him. The love of his grandmother, sister, and Andrea, helped to uproot some of that negativity. On the positive side, Magnus was more determined than ever to be an exceptional husband and father, which he came close to being. However, that bitterness had, thus far, kept him from reaching exceptional status. Submitting his heart and will to God, and totally let go of that anger for his dad, was the last major obstacle. Deep down, he wanted to get rid of that emotion. The irony was that Magnus longed to follow in his dad's career footsteps. *Why?* Magnus wasn't sure. He had many unresolved issues. Dorcus and Andrea were a blessing from the Lord for Magnus. They kept him motivated to continue in the right direction.

In many ways, Robert Steele was the opposite of Magnus. There's not much known about his younger years. From the day he walked into the CIA, there was an aura of invincibility. He was always impeccably dressed and groomed. It was GQ meets Rambo. Unlike Magnus, Robert was never a devoted family man. He loved, or liked, many women, and most of them loved him. His charm, good looks, and style were hard to resist. However, in a way, he envied Magnus. Robert greatly admired and respected Magnus's commitment as a husband and father. There was a void in his heart that all the flings with gorgeous women couldn't fill. During the course of their relationship, Robert told Magnus not to mess things up with his family. Magnus listened.

CHAPTER 5

THE UNTHINKABLE

In forty-nine days, top leaders, including the presidents from China, Russia, and the United States, would have an unprecedented meeting to discuss, of all things, nuclear weapons proliferation. The three superpowers would try to reach an agreement not to obliterate each other, and probably the world. The gathering was initiated and organized by the United Sates. The G8 Summit in Paris was the venue.

When Muslov Deshnue read an article in the *Washington Post* about Miles Williams, he was very intrigued. Not only was Miles, according to the story, a committed member of the White House security team, or Secret Service, but a model citizen in the Washington DC community because of his dedication to serving poor neighborhoods through various charities. For security reasons, the article contained no details about Williams' work, however, a name was all Deshnue needed. He hacked and dug into computer files, learning more and more about this trusted Security agent. Deshnue had moved to DC a few years before in order to instigate his plan. He knew it would take much time and patience, which Muslov had.

He easily landed a job as a computer programmer with a large company. His incredible intellect and knowledge with computer programs enabled him to progress within Dynomated World Wide. Since his background was clean, according to Dynomated's security process, he was able to achieve high levels of defense access. Years before, he'd anticipated this moment; therefore, he was careful to maintain a spotless record. This plan was in his twisted mind for many years. He was extremely competent and professional. While he was unsociable and somewhat distant, he was friendly enough not to cause suspicion. No one knew anything about his personal life. He didn't cultivate any close friendships. He always had a ready, legitimate excuse for not accepting offers to go to lunch, come to parties or play softball with the department. By design, by stealth, he blended in. Deshnue's supervisors marveled at, and loved, his accomplishments and expertise. He made them look good for the Senior Leadership. Whenever a dog and pony show came through the Information Technology Department with Dynomated top executives, the first thing area heads did was take them to Muslov's office and show off their superstar. His immaculate, neatly organized work space was full of awards. They bragged about him being the first one to arrive to work and the last to leave, and doing the same on weekends. He obliged with a convincing, fake act of charm and wit. He was the cover story of the monthly company magazine once, and eventually a contributing writer; he was the complete opposite of the messy, crazy-eyed mad genius living in a freezing, remote place. He was still that man on the inside.

Fortunately for the world, the Central Intelligence Agency is much more thorough at gathering clues and personal information than Dynomated World Wide. In the director's office, Robert, Magnus, and the director himself listened to an extensive briefing on Muslov Deshnue. It started in 2002. Local authorities in Lazo confiscated some information off of one of Deshnue's computers. While the KGB dismissed the ideas they found as impossible and laughable, his intentions were suspect. His aspirations, along with his incredible intelligence and his breakthrough research, were why the CIA was taking this threat seriously. Their biggest concern: Is it too late? The latest intelligence shows that he's in the United States. Would he go to a major city, or an obscure little town in the Mid-West? The director guessed he'd start in a secluded place to further his plan, and maybe be close to the site of a nuclear warhead. Maybe he would want to be close to a naval base in order to try something with a ship containing a nuclear pay load. Robert had a hunch Deshnue would cut right to the chase. Muslov was in Washington DC, so he believed Muslov didn't want to waste any time. His plan had already been formulated. Every shred of information about this mad genius had been thoroughly read by Steele. If anyone understood him, it was Joshua.

How did Robert know Muslov Deshnue was in Washington DC? While searching Deshnue's dwelling in Lazo, Robert was particularly interested in what was in the charred remains in the pot belly stove. There were a few pieces of paper that were not completely consumed. However, the few words that could be made out didn't mean much to the other agents, except for Robert. He carefully extracted the brittle, small pieces of paper with tweezers.

Muslov took extensive notes tracking his research. He wrote them in notebooks. Then, to reinforce his findings in his mind, he transferred his paper notes into electronic ones. He was a multitasker. After the transcription was complete from a notebook, he would throw it into the stove to help stoke the flames to battle the frigid Siberian cold.

What scraps didn't burn completely? What words could Robert discern? The following: "superpower" and "most powerful nat." This, in fact, was not much to go on. However, there was one other compelling scrap for Robert. It was thicker than paper—a notebook covering. It was rust color, with what looked like a lettering in yellow/gold. It was maybe I, H, J, K, L, M, N, P, R, or U. James narrowed it down to I, K, N, or R. Then he knew the colors. They were the rust and gold of the Washington Redskins of the National Football League. *Was Deshnue genuinely interested in football, or did he think it would behoove him to become knowledgeable about the sport, specifically the Redskins?* The local post office proved to be a wealth of information for Robert.

Through records, he learned that someone—in Lazo, Siberia, mind you—ordered a Washington Redskins' Fan Kit. Next, above one of the computers, scribbled on the wall, was the sentence: *To kill the snake, you must cut off the head.* Finally, Robert went back to the local post office. He discovered that, under a fake name, Deshnue ordered a map of Washington DC from a company in Moscow.

In this particular department of the Central Intelligence Agency, the Unconventional Terrorism Department, they took the odd cases that no one else wanted for fear of the unknown—science fiction quality. In the UTD, *Joshua* has always stood for the A+ agent: esteem, honor, and above all, success. Steele had held this title, without rival, for a quarter of a century. Magnus didn't grasp the magnitude of being considered the next Joshua.

Magnus said, "Without a doubt, given his expertise, he's changed his identity."

He did. Everyone at Dynomated knew him as Nicholas Comaneci. Deshnue did not do away with his Romanian accent. He told everyone he emigrated from Russia, and he had the documentation to back it up. While he was concerned about this, he ultimately decided his accent couldn't be a piece of evidence that could track him. If it did, it would be too late. Muslov figured his plan would be too progressed. *Did he underestimate Robert Steele and Magnus Stone?* Magnus insightfully interjected that the accent could be a place to start. The director and Robert agreed. Obviously, Magnus was fully engaged and gripped by this case, opportunity, mission. Robert knew he was too; he remembered that conviction and feeling of his first operation. The director knew it also. Deep down, Magnus couldn't help but do the right thing. His commitment to humanity and service were ingrained within him. He was in; he was ready to take on Muslov Deshnue.

CHAPTER 6

MILES WILLIAMS

Miles was born in Mobile, Alabama. His father, Walter, worked on the ship docks. His mother, Sheila, was a cleaner and cook in a historic, large, downtown church. They were a loving, hard-working, Godly couple who took very good care of Miles, his two brothers, and his one sister. Miles, Michael, and Ychilindria fulfilled their parents' dreams of going to college and excelling. However, Marcus, in between Miles the oldest son, and Michael the youngest, broke their parents' heart. The lure of the street life was too hard for him to resist; this only strengthened Mile's resolve to make his parents proud. In high school, Miles stood out as a student athlete. He earned an academic and football scholarship to the University of Southern Alabama. In his senior year, he earned all-conference honors as a defensive back. He also graduated with prestige. His parents were indeed proud. Miles was glad he pleased his folks. However, it grieved him that Marcus was not in any of the pictures at his graduation. Miles graduated with a degree in education, though he would have pursued criminal justice, but his school didn't offer that program. He had a clear goal and plan. He wanted to work with the FBI. However, once he accomplished that, he had no idea he would end up protecting the president of the United States.

CHAPTER 7

MILES AND MUSLOV MEET

Through the computer, Deshnue knew much about Miles. When the opportunity presented itself, and Muslov patiently waited for it, he moved into the apartment two doors down from the Secret Service agent. After infiltrating Williams' financial data, Deshnue noticed a number of purchases at bookstores; Miles was an avid reader. Whenever their paths crossed, Muslov gave him a friendly, but not overbearing, greeting. In a word, Deshnue was "entrancing."

About four months later, while on the phone with his mom, Mrs. Williams asked him about his neighbors.

He responded, "Overall, I have good, quiet ones. There's one guy—a couple of doors down—who really seems like a nice guy. By his accent, I think he's from somewhere in Eastern Europe."

Muslov was starting to stand out in Miles' mind. The opportunity presented itself one day. Miles and Muslov had a conversation outside their apartment. It was a perfect early summer day, hot, but not too much. It was also early evening. Muslov shrewdly steered the conversation toward books. Miles was excited and intrigued with Muslov's knowledge of literature. A friendship was starting.

July first was Miles's Birthday. This was going to be special: the big three-zero. When Miles's friends, who were putting together a party for him, invited some other friends and neighbors, Nicolas Comaneci was on the list. At the party, Muslov was pleasant and witty. Everyone enjoyed him. He was able to contribute to conversations with insightful comments and questions. Through the previous conversation with Miles, which Deshnue steered toward literature, he found out Miles had never read Les

Miserables by Victor Hugo. When it was time to give the gifts, Muslov presented a hard back, unabridged version of this classic novel of lives intermingling. Miles was appreciative, touched, and eager to read it. Miles loved to learn. He was eager to comprehend new things. Another thing that fascinated Miles about Deshnue was his job and expertise with computers. Deshnue was happy to answer Miles' questions and share his knowledge with his new friend. Deshnue never missed an opportunity to go to Miles's apartment and navigate him through the deeper levels of the capabilities of his PC.

Sunday, October thirtieth was a big day. The Redskins were playing the Giants on New York's home field. Muslov invited Miles over to his apartment to watch the game and enjoy beer and pizza. Miles was looking forward to it.

CHAPTER 8

SARAJEVO TO BERLIN

2 5 September 1998 – Tension and violence between warring factions had been brewing for a long time. A particular platoon of soldiers had established a reputation for excellence. The war-ravaged nation called in this elite, light group of United States Rangers for help in their own war on terrorism. Magnus was on a C-17 headed for Bosnia and Herzegovina.

He and his squad were assigned to a dangerous sector in Sarajevo. As they walked and patrolled the streets, M4s ready, people peered at them with resentful eyes. However, some appreciated their presence. Day after day, Magnus and his men walked the mean avenues. While some business owners tried to keep their cafés and shops clean, nice, and painted, degradation was starting to swallow this part of the city. It seemed like the sun didn't shine enough, and the rain drizzled too much. It was like this for weeks. The mood was starting to get to Magnus and his men.

One night, while lying on their cots within the spares compound, the boredom was becoming obvious. Cards and crude conversation were getting old. The guys were talking about home. An unpopular bully, loud mouth Ranger named "Blaylock" said, "Please tell me that the f***ing rumors we're going home soon are f***ing true. I can't stand this f***ing place any f***ing more!"

Magnus laughed and said, "Do you realize how stupid you sound? I'm sure you're a bright dude, but 'f***ing' is the equivalent of 'duh.' So whenever you talk, whatever intelligent thing you have to say gets lost. You sound like a f***ing idiot."

"F**k you," responded Blaylock angrily while springing off his cot red faced, head and neck veins bulging, and fists clenched.

Magnus didn't flinch. Blaylock moved toward Magnus, and before he knew what hit him, Blaylock was on the concrete floor with Magnus on top of him. Magnus had a grip on Blaylock's pain pressure point in his neck, and had one knee on his chest. Blaylock was dazed and stunned. The other twenty-two guys in that cramped room were amazed at how quickly Magnus wheeled his body and legs off the cot when Blaylock was in striking distance, catching the cursing king right below the knees, and then springing on top of him. All this took less than a second. Magnus wasn't angry, and he quickly released Blaylock. Magnus held out his hand, pulled Baylock to his feet and helped him walk, slowly, back to his own bunk. Blaylock, with much labor, laid down. The legend of Magnus Stone grew.

On November 12, Stone and his fellow soldiers were doing their routine patrol. They were approaching a small grocery store owned by a man who was appreciative and friendly toward the US forces. He gave them free drinks and snacks. However, according to a certain terrorist faction, the store owner would have to pay a price for his cavorting with the enemy, and today would be the day. While not necessarily wanting to kill him, they thought a drive by shooting would shake him up and get their message across not only to him, but to others who were thinking about being nice to their foes.

At approximately 1640 hours, a small, unassuming car rounded the corner, coming toward the shop, Magnus, a woman, and a child who were planning on going into the store. It was cold, gray, and rainy. There was minimal activity on the block. Magnus knew that people who showed support to anti-terrorist efforts could potentially be targets, even though nothing like this had happened, yet. Magnus was always alert; however, he was a little more anticipatory when he went by this particular store. While he was scanning the sector, his eyes turned toward the approaching car while the window was lowering. As he raised his rifle, an AK 47 muzzle and a flash appeared at the same time from the partially open car window. Magnus released a burst of hot lead into the car, probably wounding or killing at least the shooter, but the car managed to speed off while Magnus's comrades shot at it.

Magnus quickly ordered for the area to be secured, and then, he ordered for an assessment of the casualties. When he almost immediately noticed a person on the ground in front of the store, he called for a medic and started to use his combat lifesaving skills on the victim. However, there was nothing that could be done for the woman, a mother. Magnus was so focused on maintaining situational awareness and trying to save the casualties, he barely noticed the crying, grieving little girl clutching her dead parent. Subconsciously though, Magnus etched in his mind all the details of that precious daughter forever.

***

Robert was tracking one of his nemeses: "Midas Hand," whatever he touched turned to illegal gold. He was a major player in weapons trafficking. The chase had brought him and a beautiful Norwegian spy to Berlin, Germany. They were close to finally catching him. Intelligence produced a very, very good lead. They had him cornered. Robert knew that Hand cornered was extremely dangerous. Steele was prepared, though. With his experience, expertise, the finest state-of-the-art intelligence equipment, and the most sophisticated gear and non-conventional weapons, Steele had the upper hand.

Robert staked out, studied, and restudied, Hand's security team and setup. There were eight highly trained men around the villain. On the morning of 08 September 2005, it was time to move. At 0300 hours, Robert and Audra were set to break in to the hide out and eliminate Hand, and his security team if they got in the way. The mansion that served as a hideout was in an exclusive neighborhood just outside of Berlin. The estates were large and spread out. The roads were well maintained, and the yards, meticulously manicured. The trees were big and lush, the flowers bright and beautiful, and the grass as green as one can imagine. The Hand's estate had a high brick, ivy-covered wall with a guarded gate. The gate and wall, however, posed no problem for Robert. He and Audra hovered over the house in a compact, space-age hot air balloon. They rappelled softly to the roof. Between the black balloon, black rope and their black clothes, not even their eyes were exposed. Because of their NVGs (Night Vision Goggles), silence of the balloon and their skilled rappelling, they were completely inconspicuous. Days earlier, Robert had debated whether they should land on the roof or in the yard. His first thought was to land in the yard and then disable the security alarm. However, they would almost immediately encounter security forces, and the anchor for the balloon would be easier to find on the grounds. Robert decided to touch down on the roof. Robert had thoroughly studied the type of security system used on this house. He knew it backward and forward. After quietly lowering the anchor, with gymnastic skill he and Audra worked their way to the balcony of the master bedroom. Robert had studied a copy of the blueprints for the mansion. The balcony door was unlocked, and they were in easily.

They ran into their first snag. Steele knew this was Hand's bedroom. However, though the bed was un-made, no one was in it. *Was Hand in the bathroom?* The bathroom door was open, and the light was off with no noise coming from there. They were going to have to search the house.

They carefully stepped into the hallway. There was a guard roaming. Robert's semi-automatic with silencer immediately ended his presence. Like a cat, Robert sprang toward him. He wanted to catch him before he made a thud and before his gun dropped from his hand, but the distance was too great. The dead man's weapon knocked on the wooden floor. Robert did manage to break the fall of the collapsing corpse, though.

Ten seconds later, another one slowly came up the steps. Robert and Audra were ready behind a corner. As soon as he got close to their position, Audra fired, and Robert quickly caught the falling guard and his assault rifle with little to no noise. They went room to room searching for Hand. They didn't find him. However, they found and tranquilized two more guards while they slept. Four down; four left.

They crept downstairs. Audra saw a guard and signaled to Robert. He positioned himself and gave Audra the signal to fire. Again, Robert caught his falling frame and weapon; again, there was only minimal noise. There were no more guards inside; the rest patrolled the outside perimeter. Robert and Audra found the Midas Hand asleep on a plush leather couch in the den in front of the TV.

After ending forever Midas Hand's reign of terror, the two started for the front door, thinking there were three guards remaining. Robert knew it was exactly three hundred twenty-two feet from the front door to the main gate. Robert saw a guard roaming near the entrance. Between Robert's expert marksmanship and nearly zero wind, he dropped the guard with a shot to the head. However, the guard's machine gun made a loud clank on the stone paved driveway. Robert wondered if the other two guards heard it.

One did. He didn't think it was important, but to be on the cautious side, he released the three Dobermans. The dogs quickly discovered Robert and Audra behind a bush. Robert was ready with a tranquilizing mist. The dogs stumbled and whimpered then lay down and went to sleep.

Robert decided that with only two guards left and no attack dogs, they could make it to the main gate. Robert and Audra carefully traversed the shrubs along the side of the driveway. In the distance, Audra spotted another guard. He was moving toward them, but not as if he spotted them. They ducked behind a bush. When he was in range, Robert fired. The guard fell on the grass barely making a sound. Even though there was only one sentinel left, supposedly, Robert knew better than to become over confident.

Robert knew these guards were well-trained. He was certain the remaining one would stay in his zone, or post, patrolling the backyard. However, Robert didn't want to take any chances. Using a few decorative stones that were a part of the landscaping, he hurled them at the top of a tree near the side of the house. With the rustling noise, he hoped to draw the guard to the side of the dwelling so he could know for sure where he was. It worked. From behind the back of the house, they saw him slowly move with his machine gun in the ready position. Moving back-to-back toward the main gate, Audra faced the exit, while Robert moved backwards, keeping his eyes on the alert guard. They were separated from him by approximately seventy-five yards. The sentry didn't move any further. He was disciplined enough not to stray too far from his zone.

When they were ten feet from the gate, whizzing sounds and a sharp, burning pain roared through Robert's right shoulder at the same time. He immediately went to the ground and looked to the right. He identified a guard fifty feet away, locked in—with extreme difficulty because of his wounded shoulder—and killed him. Audra was lying on her back, motionless. Robert checked her pulse. Her open, empty eyes said it all. She was killed instantly with a round to the head. Where did the ninth guard come from? That question would forever haunt Robert Steele—code name: "Joshua."

Chapter 9

GAME DAY

When Miles walked into Muslov's apartment, he was immediately struck by how sparse it was. There was a plain, cloth couch, a nice forty-two inch flat-screen television, and nothing else—no pictures. Jokingly, Miles said, "Uh, bro, are you like a monk or what?"

"It's a work in progress," Deshnue responded, smiling. "Now, let's get down to business. Make yourself comfortable, enjoy the pre-game show, I think they call it, and I'll get the beer and pizza." With that, Muslov went into the kitchen. Deshnue put a couple of pieces of pizza on a plate, pulled a beer from the refrigerator and removed the top. To make sure Miles was still in his place, he loudly said, "The Giants are looking good so far, huh?" While Miles responded, still sitting on the couch, Muslov took a small vile from the cabinet and emptied the contents into Miles's brew. He then served the pizza and beer to his guest. After getting his beverage and pepperoni slice, Muslov settled on the couch, acting like he was interested in the analysis on the upcoming game, and the NFL season. He was fighting to conceal the anxious excitement for what may happen after Miles fully succumbed to the sleeping medication. His roughly quarter of a century old obsessive plan was on the verge of being implemented.

Miles felt drowsy all of the sudden. He put the half eaten pizza and the more than half consumed beer on the floor. He crossed his arms and settled comfortably into the corner of the couch. Then, he gave in and leaned his head back. He was asleep within minutes. Now, Deshnue was calm and focused, reminiscent of the way he acted when he received that call in 1979. He quietly walked into the kitchen, pulled a syringe out of the drawer and another vile out of the refrigerator. He injected a stronger tranquilizer to ensure that Miles would be virtually comatose for about three or four hours. He put Miles over his shoulder in a fireman's carry and took him into one of the bedrooms. There were three PCs, a four-by-two-by-three feet mainframe, two reclining chairs side by side, a bundle of wires, which in the dark looked like a den of snakes, and two helmets that looked like the kind used in virtual reality experiences. A thick wire connected the top of the helmets to the mainframe. Deshnue put Miles in one of the chairs in the reclined position. He secured the helmet on him. It took him eleven minutes to type in the necessary data. Muslov had approximately eight seconds after hitting the Enter button for the last time to be in the other chair with his helmet positioned. He executed this quickly and flawlessly. For sixty-six minutes and six seconds, both men twitched and convulsed.

When it was done, Muslov fell trying to get out of the chair because he was so disoriented. After a couple of minutes, he struggled to his hands and knees, then to his feet. He staggered and stumbled to a chair. He sat with his head in his hands for a few minutes, periodically shaking his head and opening his eyes wide to try and clear the cobwebs. He got up and walked around for about a minute, waiting to feel like he could pick up Miles again and put him back in the same position on the couch. Moments later, Miles was in the same spot where he drifted off to sleep. It was complete. Deshnue executed the seemingly impossible: Being in two places at one time.

Miles slowly woke up to the sound of a prime-time cartoon. The game was long finished. Miles opened his eyes wide, shook his head, stretched, and did everything to wake from a deep sleep. He was confused, but he had two agonizing feelings: He was drugged, and he was very uncomfortable being in Deshnue's presence. The friendship was over. Since Muslov was in control, the ploy was finished; he didn't have to act nice anymore. He calmly and quietly told Miles to leave. Miles couldn't get out of there fast enough. The crisp air outside helped Miles wake fully.

Did Nicholas drug me? Did he violate me sexually? Miles was relieved that there was no physical discomfort or symptoms of such perversion. Miles had to shake it off and start preparing for an important trip to Paris in a week.

CHAPTER 10
HUNT FOR MUSLOV DESHNUE

The search came to Washington DC. They agreed to start with agencies, companies, and organizations with the most sophisticated computer capacities. The Science and Technology Department at the CIA came up with a list of the specifications needed to support Deshnue's requirements. The list has 373 such necessities. Twelve investigating agents were deployed to interview thousands of people to find a suspect.

Magnus had a strong idea as well. He suggested going to the power companies, and get a list of residents with unusually high power surges in and around the DC area. An agent was immediately on it. This produced a list of 1,866 leads in and around the DC area. Twelve agents, disguised as Potomac Electric Power Company technicians, worked day and evening going from home to home. All but twenty-seven had legitimate hobbies or side jobs that required incredible amounts of electricity. Robert and Magnus divided up the twenty-seven. Robert, wearing a PEPC uniform, knocked on Muslov's door at 2017 hours, Thursday, November 3. Robert immediately picked up on the Romanian accent. He explained that Deshnue's residence was using so much juice, and he needed to inspect the premises again for safety. Robert was even more suspicious when the villain demanded proper identification, which he produced.

Muslov escorted Robert from room to room. The main bedroom was a mess. On the floor was a twin mattress, a sleeping bag, and books and manuals on computer programming and psychology. Muslov stammered and said, "I just moved in." Robert considered making small talk about the reading material, but decided silence would be the best approach. When in doubt, don't say anything.

When they passed by the second bedroom, Robert paused, but Deshnue kept walking. When Muslov realized that Steele had stopped in front of the closed door, waiting to enter, he said, more composed and smiling, "Oh, that room is worse than the main bedroom. Most of my belongings are in there. If my slave-driving boss ever gives me some time; I'll organize this place better. I don't have anything connected to outlets in there."

With that, Robert smiled and nodded, then courteously exited the apartment. When he was at a distance that he could still see Deshnue's apartment and knew the suspect couldn't see him, he called for two agents immediately. After they arrived, Steele instructed them to tail the man living in apartment number eleven, and if he went to the airport, train station, bus station, rental car agency, or started driving with the intent of leaving the city, stop him.

Through old photos the CIA obtained of Deshnue, and computer generation, they compiled a book full of pictures of what the madman could look like, including all possible alterations. Unless Muslov underwent complete facial reconstructive surgery, this manual contained a picture of him. Deshnue opted for a closely buzzed hair style, with a beard and mustache of equal length. They had all turned from strawberry blonde to gray, but he dyed them black. He used hazel tinted contacts to cover his natural brown eyes. The manual entitled *Sixty-Seven Possible Looks Alterations of Muslov Deshnue* held a nearly exact replica of the new antihero. He couldn't change his seventy three inch, slightly hunched, medium frame.

Back at headquarters, the CIA team was prepared to brief on what they discovered. One agent briefed on a man who fit the profile at Dynamated World Wide. He presented company magazine pictures of Nicholas Comaneci and was compelled by

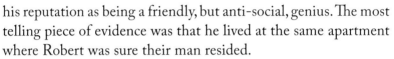

his reputation as being a friendly, but anti-social, genius. The most telling piece of evidence was that he lived at the same apartment where Robert was sure their man resided.

Finally, Muslov hadn't noticed Robert's sleight of hand with a piece of fingerprint lifting tape on the inside of his left digits. Robert inconspicuously put his hand on a door knob right after Muslov grabbed it. The agent who combed Nicholas Comaneci's office found clear fingerprint samples one night after the employee was gone, and the two patterns matched.

Robert didn't even give his portion of the briefing. He heard and saw all he needed. He moved with a definite sense of purpose toward the door and said, "Let's go. We have him. The director knew not to question Steele when he had that look and sound of resolve. The director would work his CIA and FBI connections for a warrant later if necessary. Time was of the essence.

Sunday, November 6, at 1033 hours, the CIA descended on Deshnue's apartment. Two agents quietly positioned themselves behind the gate of Muslov's small, fenced patio. With stealth, Robert and Magnus approached his front door. Two other agents were behind separate bushes twenty feet away. They were all wearing casual clothes so as not to draw attention. Robert slid a small, black apparatus out of his pocket. It was a box with four thick needles next to each other and protruding out two inches. He inserted the needles into the two locks, and in seconds, they were compromised. Robert nodded to Magnus, opened the door, and Stone moved in with his 9MM in the ready position. He caught a glimpse of Deshnue dashing into the kitchen. Magnus sprang into that room, and ended up on one knee with his pistol pointed at Muslov.

Deshnue didn't have a gun, but he held a syringe he had grabbed out of the refrigerator. He was about to jab himself in the leg. Magnus shot forward and secured his wrist with the needle about an inch from the desperate madman's thigh. Deshnue was not adept to hand-to-hand combat. Magnus had little trouble, even with one hand holding a pistol, pinning Muslov face down on the floor. Two agents were right there to bind his wrists and ankles with plastic straps. Each one took an arm, lifted him to his feet, and sat him on the couch per Robert's orders. Robert knew Muslov wouldn't talk, so he wasn't going to waste time asking him questions. Robert calmly said, "I wonder why you were trying to kill yourself or sedate yourself out. My guess is you think it's possible for someone to figure out your plan and possibly thwart it."

Deshnue responded with a cocky grin, "No one, no one can decode my years of master planning and work." The incredible genius didn't know about the equally intellectually talented Wilmington "Will" Vanderburgh.

Ever since Muslov Deshnue appeared on the CIA radar screen, Will was on the case. His passion for computers and science matched Muslov's. The only difference was that his obsession was for good. Like Deshnue, he slept for a few hours on a cot in his computer science lab. He ate while he worked. He only left to use the bathroom, shower, when a family member begged for him to, or when a superior ordered him out to get some fresh air and sunshine. Even then, work was constantly on his mind. Will proudly proclaimed himself a computer geek. Many in the CIA knew him by his trademark hiking boots, jeans, and t-shirt. He bragged about never buying t-shirts. His parents were retired and traveled the country in an RV, and they always bought their beloved son a new t-shirt from a tourist destination. His medium-brown, uncombed hair and thin, wire rim glasses were a permanent fixture. He had a quirky sense of humor, with the ability to laugh at his own frequent absent mindedness. On this particular day, he was wearing his Mount Rushmore t-shirt.

Will stood in the doorway of Deshnue's bedroom converted into a lab, looking around and nodding. He was armed with his over-weighted backpack and suitcase on rollers. They were both filled with manuals, binders, and notebooks full of data he scribed over the months. Will sat down at Muslov's computer, armed with energy drinks. He knew even if he successfully got in, it would possibly take a while. Once the area and Deshnue were secure, agents brought in duffle bags, sleeping bags, cots, a cooler of bottled waters, and military MRE's. They were prepared for the long haul as well.

Robert wasn't going to transport Muslov. He fully intended to do the interrogation at Muslov's headquarters. Steele started by getting comfortable and turning on the television. He told the other agents to relax. Magnus wasn't sure about this. He was ready to play the bad cop and speed up this process. As he glared at Deshnue, he said, "Why don't you let me beat the information out of him?" Robert was seated on the couch next to the villain with his head leaned back. He slightly rolled it toward Muslov and asked, "Would it work if he rearranged your face?" Deshnue silently stared. Robert gave Muslov a lengthy brief on Wilmington Vanderburgh. It took quite a few minutes. His education achievements are extremely impressive. Deshnue had a blank stare. He was somewhere else, literally. He was still getting used to being in two places at one time.

Ever since that fateful day in Deshnue's apartment, Miles felt very strange and light headed; his sleep was labored. Muslov constantly invaded his dreams. He had to focus, though. He had to prepare for the biggest assignment of his career: Guarding the President of the United States while he met with other world leaders. Strange, however, the thought frequently flashed across his mind to kill one of them. Why? He was a basically kind, loving person. He didn't hate anyone. He wasn't a political activist. He had his views like everyone else, but he always managed to keep them in perspective. The evil in Muslov Deshnue's soul was beginning to consume Mile's being.

Back at the apartment, the hours started to pass as Will worked feverishly on Muslov's computer. In the living room, Deshnue finally broke his silence and said, "It's too late. Even if this inferior Wilmington character figures out what I'm doing, it will be finished." The partially mad man reflected and laughed with pleasure at his wit and concluded, "Didn't Jesus say something like that?"

It was finally time to sleep. The agents took shifts watching Muslov. Robert checked on Will. He gently asked, "Progress, Will the Thrill?"

Will responded without taking his eyes off the screen, "Slow, Sir."

Robert asked, "What's your favorite MRE?"

Will grinned and looked at Steele, "The vegetarian black bean burrito, Sir."

As Robert turned and started for the living room he said with a dignified air, "One exquisite vegetarian black bean burrito coming up, Sir." Will's grin intensified as he watched the screen.

The password to get into Deshnue's computer was relatively easy. He used, *Boris1979RIP*. It took Will a couple of hours to figure this out. The technical calculations weren't difficult for the young scientist either. The struggle came in getting into Muslov's head—thinking like an evil man. Having to do this was wearing down the basically innocent and sweet natured Wilmington Vanderburgh, but he persevered, knowing he had to do it so good could prevail.

At one point, Robert looked around the living room. Magnus was lying on his back on top of his sleeping bag. Two agents were curled up on one layer of their military, three layered, sleeping bag. The fourth agent guarded Muslov, who was leaned over on the side of the couch, awake with his feet on the floor. Robert ordered that his hands be re-bound in the front so he could lie on his back and be more comfortable. At this, without moving,

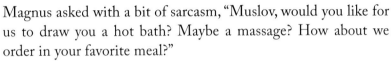

Magnus asked with a bit of sarcasm, "Muslov, would you like for us to draw you a hot bath? Maybe a massage? How about we order in your favorite meal?"

Joshua immediately ordered the young Mr. Stone out onto the back patio after Deshnue was re-secured. Robert faced the glass door so he could keep one eye on the captive. In a low voice, he scolded the impatient future superstar agent on the need for patience and on the negative effect of insubordination. Robert concluded with the most compelling reason of all: "There are a lot of unknowns here. Are we going to have to travel through this scary, demented man's mind? It'll probably be horrid enough. I don't want to add to the difficulty by having him sleep deprived. Ultimately, we do not torture. and we always, always do the right thing. Regardless of the pressure to expedite the process, we must rise above our base instincts. In my forty plus years of service to humanity through the CIA, I've come to realize that, in the end, doing the scrupulous thing wins the day." Magnus nodded and sincerely apologized.

As Robert walked back in, he felt he needed to ease the tension. He searched the apartment for cleaning supplies for the bathroom. Muslov's ablution habits left much to be desired. Robert's men always respected him because he led from the front. He was willing to be a servant, even clean a shower and toilet. No matter where he was in the apartment, he spoke loud enough so that all could hear: "A number of years ago we had a similar situation of camping out in a criminal's home. He was a sheikh that lived in a palace in Saudi Arabia. He had maids that kept the accommodations immaculate. Unfortunately, Mr. Deshnue is a poor living criminal master mind." One agent who was with Robert on that mission laughed as he reminisced.

Robert didn't get very far in the quest and story. A blurry eyed Will, leaning against the doorway of the bedroom said, "I got it." His enthusiasm was tempered with the fear of the unknown.

CHAPTER 11

HUNT FOR MUSLOV DESHNUE: PART II

"What's the next step, Agent Vanderburgh?" Robert asked. "Put Deshnue in one of these chairs and put the helmet on him. One of us will have to do the same simultaneously in the other recliner," responded Will warily.

They were in a tough spot. Robert knew time was not on their side. However, he also realized they needed to be deliberate on choosing who would go. Should Will go because of his knowledge? He was an eager volunteer. No, he needed to be at the helm on this side. Magnus? Robert didn't like that idea because of his wife and baby girl. One of the agents, like Will, had expertise that required him to stay on this side; he was a trained medic, and whoever went needed constant monitoring. Robert was not comfortable with the other two agents because of lack of experience or a proven track record. Robert, ever leading from the front, would go. Magnus requested a word with Robert privately, back on the back patio.

Stone started. "An extra set of ears, eyes, and hands could be very valuable. I'm grateful for your genuine concern for my fatherhood, but Andrea knows full well the potential risks. She supports what we do." Robert listened intently. The brave Mr. Stone continued, "Besides, she has a strong connection to the Divine." Robert's eyebrows rose. Magnus finished, "If I die, she and Dawn will be in good hands. She's been praying for us—for you—constantly, and she'll continue to do so. I'm not sure why I'm telling you, or what it means, but I found it somewhat comforting.

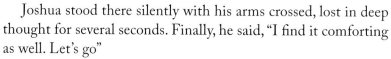

Joshua stood there silently with his arms crossed, lost in deep thought for several seconds. Finally, he said, "I find it comforting as well. Let's go"

As Deshnue was being taken to the makeshift lab, he resisted for the first time. He was jerking and twisting. He cursed and yelled, "It's too late!" Two agents had to hold Muslov down in the chair. Will put the helmet on him. Will then looked at Robert with grave concern in his eyes, and then he looked at the other chair. Robert understood the non-verbal communication. He completely unbuttoned his shirt while he settled in. One of the agents attached monitoring wires to his chest, and Will carefully placed the other helmet on his head. The heart and respiratory monitors were set. Robert nodded at Will. There was no need for a briefing. No one knew what to expect. With much concern, Will started working the keyboard.

Days before, the talented young Mr. Vanderburgh gave a thorough presentation on his extensive research. It was a jam packed, three hour seminar. It went by quickly, though. Everyone was enthralled, Robert and Magnus the most. Will explained his theory on body, soul, spirit, and the subconscious. He documented the cases of outer carcass experiences, proposing the possibility of a person being in two places at one time. He said that the spirit can detach from the physical body; hence, people seeing themselves on the hospital bed, for example.

Vanderburgh stated that the mind, the subconscious, is the portal for transporting between body and spirit. Via a complex, computed formula, Deshnue figured out how to use a computer program to act as a conduit—in other words, a traffic signal, or floodgate. Will also used the example of a penitentiary: A guard at a control panel manipulates which doors are unlocked and opened. The mind is like the prison. Deshnue, and now Will, are similar to the guards at the control board, controlling the apertures, and allowing the spirit to travel to different places. It's obviously more complicated than that. Dr. Vanderburgh, who earned his doctorate at the age of twenty-three, was breaking it down into simple terms. He didn't necessarily need to for Robert, but he did for the others.

Robert and Deshnue began to twitch and convulse with their eyes still open. After approximately sixty-six minutes, they both laid still with blank stares. Where was Joshua? Robert was helped out of the chair and laid on a cot. Magnus didn't want to wait to ask him about his experience; he wanted to be with his comrade and mentor. He quickly sat in the chair and placed the helmet on his head. In a calm, composed tone, he said to Will, "Hurry."

As Magnus felt himself fade, the light in the room grew bigger until it totally consumed him. He felt like he was confined to an invisible seat. He couldn't move. He felt very awake again. The trip was like a roller coaster except he couldn't see the next curve or hump. There was nothing but an intense white light, initially; then the light slowly faded to a gray. The worst part was that, unlike a regular roller coaster that lasts two to three and a half minutes, this one went on for over an hour. The team was concerned about Deshnue's health. After two trips, his vital signs were racing, and he was sweating profusely. They gave him an injection to slow his heart rate.

Finally, Magnus was flung onto a sidewalk. It took him a few minutes to get his wits. When he was on his feet, he looked around. He was in a hazy world of faded colors. He finally recognized that street in Sarajevo where his worst mission took place. He looked back from the area from where he was ejected. It was a circle of pulsating light, which was approximately eight feet in diameter. It was in front of his favorite shopkeeper's store.

When he turned back toward the street, it was gone. He was now on a tarmac fifty feet away from Air Force One. As he walked toward the stairs to enter the President of the United States' plane, an ominous, giant figure swept in front of him and blocked his way. It was the silhouette of a hooded, robed figure. However, it was one dimensional. It, or he, was about eight feet tall. It was as if it was hollow. Looking at it was like peering through a hole. It was beyond black. It was like a cave miles underground, with absolutely no light. Then, Magnus noticed dozens of smaller ones, five feet tall, flying around, circling him. As fear started to seize him, he whispered, "Please help me, God." With that, the demon let out a low, soft, but nevertheless, blood curling shriek. It also shuttered. At this, Magnus's fear subsided. As he moved toward the demon in order to get to the stairs, it moved aside, allowing the future Joshua to pass. When Magnus put his hand on the stair rail, he was taken aback. It was not his hand, but rather, a dark brown hand of someone from African lineage. Before he even had time to question this strange occurrence, the earth gave way beneath his feet. He was free falling from the sky. In the midst of his terror from such a happening, the smaller demons were swirling around him. They were bellowing hideous laughter. He also noticed, whirling about him, the woman who was shot and killed in Sarajevo and her crying daughter. By instinct, he cried out to God again. At that moment, his descent slowed rapidly until he gently alighted on the ground. The little girl did the same, however, the dead mother hit the ground hard. It sent shivers through every part of his body. How long will this haunt him? Magnus couldn't bear to look at either one of them. He stood with his back to them, and his face in his right hand. He felt the unmistakable touch of a gentle, soft, small child's hand take a hold of his left one. He looked down at the little angel. With all the innocence that only a small child can muster, she looked up at him and said, "It wasn't your fault. The bad men did it. You tried to help."

Magnus kneeled beside her. With the perfect combination of gentleness and strength, he hugged her. While tears formed in his eyes, he whispered over and over, "I'm sorry."

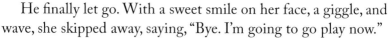

He finally let go. With a sweet smile on her face, a giggle, and wave, she skipped away, saying, "Bye. I'm going to go play now."

As Magnus watched her go, the eight-foot tall demon moved in front of him. The prince of darkness was holding the woman's body in one hand like a rag doll. He held her in front of Magnus's face. Then the demon looked over his shoulder and said, in a very intelligent sounding, dignified voice, "The splendid innocence of children; a lovely *corporeality*." He looked up at his imps hovering overhead and nodded in the direction of where the little girl had gone. They immediately took off after her.

Magnus instinctively sprinted to save her, but he felt like he was running in neck-deep water. The sinking feeling hit him that he could not get there in time. Again, without thinking, he whispered, "Please protect her God."

After being exhausted and barely able to move, he noticed his surroundings for the first time since his free fall. He was in a particular field of Texas Bluebonnets. His dad took him there when he was seven. To his right, about ten feet away, there was a small patch of fog. In the fog, there appeared to be a small window. As Magnus approached it, he noticed that it was, in fact, a window. It was head-high, exactly one-foot-by-one-foot. It was suspended in midair. It was open, and he cautiously looked through it. He was back in the makeshift lab. He saw a couple of the agents sitting to the side and the back of Will's head.

He asked, "Can you hear me?"

With a bit of a start, all three turned around. By their reaction, he knew he was back in the conscious world. Anxiously, one of the agents asked, "What have you seen?"

"Demons, things from my past, and Air Force One. Any word from Robert?"

Will responded, "Yes, He's come back to us twice; he's experienced basically the same things you have. He told us to share with you that controlling your fear seems to prevent the demons from attacking. What details do you recall from Air Force One?"

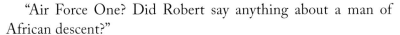

"Air Force One? Did Robert say anything about a man of African descent?"

"He was on board, and it was flying. That's all he could recall," responded one of the agents.

"I saw it still on a tarmac. I went to climb the stairs into the cabin, and my hand was like a black man's. That's it. I'm off again." With that, the physical Magnus had a blank stare again.

When he turned away from the window, he was on a city street. It appeared a little dirtier, duller, and older than a modern city. The people seemed downcast. Magnus guessed it to be a city in the former Soviet Union, a Baltic city maybe. As he scanned the faces, he saw Muslov. When their eyes met, Deshnue started running through the crowd on the sidewalk. Magnus gave chase. But again, the sluggish, slow motion feeling overtook him. However, he noticed the same phenomenon appeared to be happening to Muslov. Magnus had a chance to catch him. Magnus was gaining on him. He was going to overtake Deshnue! Suddenly, a bunch of demons picked up Muslov and whisked him away.

As Magnus stood there with his hands on his hips, exhausted and discouraged, he heard the voice from behind, "Valiant effort young man!" He turned around and was immediately looking into the black hole mid-section of the prince of demons. "You gave it all you had, but you couldn't apprehend Deshnue. It wasn't even contiguous. Word of advice: give it up. This is a dangerous place. You have no idea really. Here, let me give you a small snippet, a taste, if you will." With that, the demon snapped his fingers.

Instantly, the demon was gone, and in front of Magnus, fifty feet out, he saw a flash. Before he could react, there was a bullet suspended in midair, hovering right between his eyes an inch away. "Now, brave young Magnus, I could have allowed the bullet to finish," came the demon's voice from behind. "Turn around please. Allow me to brandish something else." From around its back he presented the dead mother. This time he was holding her corpse more gently in one arm. He slowly passed his left hand over her face. It changed to Andrea! Magnus felt his knees buckle. The demon put his hollow hand on Magnus's shoulder and said, "Come with me friend." He started to walk the numb young man down the street. He continued to gently carry the dead body.

"This line of work is much too risky for a committed family man such as yourself; not only the perpetual danger to you, but the inherent peril to lovely Andrea and precious Dawn. If it weren't for this hazardous mission, you could be with them right now." With his now empty left hand, the prince of demons gestured toward the right side.

There they were, Magnus, Andrea, and Dawn in the park close to their home. Dawn giggled in the swing as Magnus gently pushed her from behind and mom pushed her from the front. Mom and dad had very content, happy smiles. Magnus was mesmerized, watching himself in action. It was almost like observing a home movie. The demon stood silently, allowing Magnus to fully take in the sight and emotions.

"Austin is a nice, relatively safe city, friend," the evil presence continued. "You could get on the police force there, get the seven to three shift and be home by three thirty or four. You'd have the rest of the day and night with your loving family. It's a shame really you're missing out on little Dawn's cute years. Did you know she's learned two new words since you've been gone?" Magnus was glassy eyed. "Let's face it, young man, your wife is a very pretty, desirable woman. Many Texas men have noticed and want her. There is one now who is beguiling her, trying to play on her deep down loneliness" Hopefully Magnus will remember his grandmother's saying, "Sin uses just enough truth to sweeten the Grand Lie." The demon continued, "A wife needs her man there—not to mention the angst and worry she deals with concerning your mission. You were deployed two times with the Army, incarcerated once—shame on you, gone weeks for your

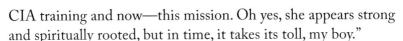

CIA training and now—this mission. Oh yes, she appears strong and spiritually rooted, but in time, it takes its toll, my boy."

This time, the demon gestured to the left. It was a scene from Tikrit, Iraq in 2003. Magnus was in the thick of the action on a dismounted foot patrol extracting Insurgents. On this particular day, an RPG (Rocket Propelled Grenade) whizzed about a foot by his head. It hit a wall and exploded fifteen feet from him. Magnus sustained minor wounds from shrapnel and pieces of the palisade. He never missed Andrea so much in his whole life. The emotions of that day came flooding back to Magnus while he watched as a spectator this time.

As they proceeded down the street, the prince waved his hand toward the right. The scene was from a forest in the former Yugoslavia. In 1999, as he and his squad marched through the trees, they came under sniper fire. Magnus yelled, "Contact, two o'clock," as he dropped and rolled behind a tree. About twenty feet ahead, Magnus saw and heard his buddy lying on the ground. He was barely moving, and he was moaning. Magnus knew he had been shot. Despite the crack and whiz sounds, he sprang to his feet. While bent low, he ran to his comrade, grabbed him, and pulled him behind some hardwood. He did what he could to attend the wound, and then, he started returning fire. They eventually eliminated the threat; however, it was too late for Magnus's friend. Once again, Magnus couldn't wait to embrace his wife.

The relationship between Andrea and Magnus began with high drama. They were destined to be an adventurous family to say the least. Andrea was a very special, rare woman. She knew, and accepted, the risks of Magnus's calling. Their marriage is safe. However, the demon was doing an effective job of planting seeds of doubt in the future Joshua's mind, or the man who could be the future Joshua.

"Shall we continue, young man? You see, it's obvious this isn't the life for a swain with a lovely wife and sweet little girl, and I'm

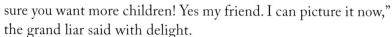

sure you want more children! Yes my friend. I can picture it now," the grand liar said with delight.

The demon waved his hand to the left. The scene was the family's quaint, old Presbyterian Church. Dorcus had originally started attending there almost a half a century ago. They were all standing in front with the minister. The Godly, aged Dorcus looked dignified; Magnus made a rare appearance in a coat and tie; Andrea looked sweet but stunning; and Dawn, a little older, was the cutest child in the world in her light pink dress, bow, sweater, and black shoes. Andrea was holding a tiny baby wrapped in a light blue blanket. It was the baptism of Magnus's son. The family looked so content. Dorcus was overwhelmed with pride. Her eyes were moist. Even though she couldn't see clearly, she felt and knew exactly what was happening.

Magnus's eyes were red and swollen as he watched. "Son," started the prince of darkness as he put his pseudo-hand on the sad hero's shoulder, "this work is fine for Robert and the director. They're not committed family men. Despicable really; they're deceiving you into joining this high risk lifestyle. I'm indignant for you."

Evil always speaks too much. This last sentence brought Magnus back to reality. He didn't trust the demon, and he didn't want him to be "indignant" for him. He also remembered the picture on the director's desk of his wife, children, and grandchildren. Still, the demon did successfully plant doubt in Magnus. Was all this worth it, especially when he could be with his wife and Daddy's girl? Magnus was starting to come to his senses. "I doubt you'll be forthright, but why are you showing me all this?" Magnus knew he—it had an ulterior motive.

After a pensive pause, the demon explained: "Granted, young man, I am evil. You know that. You're very smart. I have to pick and choose wisely how I'm going to deceive you, but what I've shown you are simply scenes from the past, right? And the last thing is something you aspire and long for, true? I've only shown

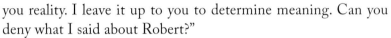

you reality. I leave it up to you to determine meaning. Can you deny what I said about Robert?"

Magnus, stronger and more resolved, "Why are you distracting me from finding Muslov? Of course, you won't tell me the truth." Magnus recalled Robert's message not to fear these demons. With greater fortitude, he said, "I want the little girl."

Now, not looking so big, the demon said, "Okay, my friend, but what will you render to me in return?" He called to the sky and ordered down a few of his archfiends.

Magnus, now in control, said, "I will admit, you've given me something serious to think about. I can't deny that. I will ponder riding off into the Texas sunset and live a quiet life with my family. You're right; that is extremely appealing. However, how will I know you and your ilk won't bother us?"

Pleased, the demon responded, "You and your little family living a quiet life in Austin wouldn't pose a threat to us—deal."

"Deal?" questioned Magnus with an authoritative voice. "I said I would 'ponder.' Before we come close to a 'deal,' give me the little girl."

The demon snapped his fingers with delight. One of the imps standing about ten feet away stepped once to the side. There was the scared little girl. She ran and grabbed Magnus's leg. The prince was satisfied. He gave Magnus something to consider, and now he will be preoccupied with the girl; he was distracted from hunting Muslov.

⟶➣●꛲⟵

Over the Atlantic Ocean, Miles stared out the window of Air Force One. It was dawn. Everyone around him slept; he couldn't. He felt a rage inside him that he never felt before. One of his fellow agents, Martin Dixon, who was also a friend, had noticed a change, a difference in Miles. As Martin awakened, he noticed that Miles was not sleeping. He decided to broach the subject. "Everything alright?" Miles shot him a startled, angry look and remained silent. Martin didn't say anything else. However, he got his answer. No doubt there was something bothering Miles.

Just then, a voice came over the intercom. It was the pilot. "Good morning. We'll be in Paris in roughly four hours."

———⟫●⟪———

Magnus knelt down in order to be eye level with the little girl. In his gentle, fatherly voice, he spoke, "What's your name?"

In a soft, frightened voice, she responded, "Nadia."

"Pleased to meet you, Nadia; my name is Magnus." She gazed into his eyes and then shyly looked down. He stood, took her delicate hand, and said, "Let's go; I'm looking for my friend, Robert, and a bad person named Muslov."

Suddenly, they were floating in midair. Magnus grabbed and held Nadia close. A rumbling sound was rapidly approaching. Within seconds, Air Force One roared past them. The force of the wind draft sent them spinning out of control. Nadia screamed. They gently floated into a soft, grassy green field. It was a beautiful place, spotted with purple, red, and yellow wild flowers. It was surrounded by big, full trees, and there was not a cloud in the crisp, blue sky. Magnus thought to himself, *Where do I start to look for Robert and Deshnue?*

Nadia looked around, smiled, and said, "How pretty!"

CHAPTER 12

PLANTING SEEDS OF DOUBT IN ROBERT

Fifty yards ahead, Magnus saw the low patch of fog again. Holding Nadia's hand, he moved toward it. She wanted to make frequent stops to pick flowers. He gently said, "We have to hurry, sweetie. There will be time for picking flowers later." She complied without resistance.

As Magnus got closer, he saw the familiar window. He was anxious to check in and find out about Robert. "Hello, dudes." The agents in the room, especially Will, were pleased to hear from the fully conscious Magnus. The first thing Magnus asked, "How's Robert? Has he said anything about the…demon-like beings and Air Force One?"

Will said, "According to Robert, the so-called demon-like beings' purpose is to distract us from finding Muslov. They use any means necessary to accomplish this."

Magnus looked down at Nadia and lightly squeezed her hand. She asked, "Can I look in the window?" With a pleasant grin, Magnus shook his head.

Magnus reported, "I've had more than one encounter with Air Force One and the demons, especially the large, apparent leader. He's eight feet tall, and blacker than black itself. It's not even the color black, but a nothingness black, a void, an emptiness. He's only one-dimensional."

Will responded, "Your descriptions of the demon, or whatever he is, are almost identical. Do you have any details about your Air Force One encounter? Robert said it was flying over an ocean."

One of the other agents interjected, "In approximately eighteen hours, the G8 Summit to reduce the threat of WMD's proliferation is beginning in Paris. China and Russia have been invited as well. It is unprecedented. The President of the United States is almost there." As the four in the room glanced at each other, Robert was only partially lucid.

Magnus said, "I'd better go." When he turned, he was immediately struck by a biting, cold wind. He looked down, and Nadia was shivering. He took her in his arms, put his head down, and started walking. Between carrying Nadia, the freezing wind, and the snow he was walking through, it was very difficult. Where were they? All he knew was, wherever they currently resided, it was bitter cold, and snowy.

⟶➤●⟵

Robert was starting to get warm. He had been out of that same frigid place for about five minutes. He suspected it was Siberia. Robert had his stiffest test there. While being cold and miserable, the prince of darkness did a masterful job working on his psychological state. As expected, the demon bombarded Robert with images of that tragic night in Germany. It walked him through the three dimensional cinema, like Magnus's personal one. It was worse for Robert though. The cold was wearing down his resolve.

The first scene was a quaint, old coffee shop in Berlin. Robert and Audra sat in simple wooden chairs at an equally simple wooden table. A rich cherry-like wood-trimmed, cozy place. Weathered, cherry wood framed oil paintings of the German countryside and mountains graced the fading walls. Clouded sunlight poured through the large windows. The scent of coffee was delightful. For once, Robert felt he could give up his playboy ways. Audra had a depth of character and inner beauty that stirred untapped emotions within him. This was an awkward moment for him because he was expressing his heart to her. As Robert was sharing all this to Audra, his suave was gone. While joy and love

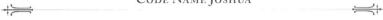

welled within her, she maintained her demeanor, and responded, "I don't think we should be talking about this during a mission. We must maintain focus." Robert stared into his tea and nodded slightly in agreement. She moved closer to him, kissed him on the cheek and smiled, saying, "Besides, you're Robert Steele. You don't settle down. I don't want a broken heart."

Robert shifted and responded, "Yes, well, Robert Steele isn't a young man anymore, and I want to settle down and have at least one child. I want someone to call me Daddy." Audra caressed and squeezed his arm. She was incredibly hopeful and touched by his transparency.

Shivering, with freezing tears in his eyes, Robert looked up at the prince of demons and said, "You went too far. Don't you see? I have nothing to live for—nothing to lose. I'll die stopping Muslov. Why not? Audra is dead. Leave me!"

Once again, evil miscalculated. Suddenly, he didn't look eight feet tall as he slinked away. The ground gave way beneath Robert. It was still gray and frigid around him as he fell. He alighted on his feet. He was inside a plush jetliner. He immediately recognized it was Air Force One. He saw the back of a man exiting through the open hatch. He believed it was the President of the United States. Robert realized that Muslov was probably going to do something at the G8 Summit. As he moved toward the door to see where they were, the airplane hatch turned into an old, simple wood door. He opened it, stepped through and looked around; he recognized the orphanage he lived in between the ages of seven and seventeen.

The distinctive smell came back to him. It invaded his nostrils like a telemarketer's call at dinner time. It was the combination of beefy vegetable soup, urine, body order, and ammonia cleaning solution. It was always clean and organized in appearance. So far, this had been the most vivid segment of Robert's exploration through this dream world. He was walking from room to room. He started in the large, main room. The walls were faded white and void of pictures, and the wood floor was dull, faded, and scuffed. The beat up furniture was pushed against the sides of the room.

Survival and thriving in Loudown Boys Home depended on being in with the right clique, or gang. Robert didn't trust any syndicate, and he definitely didn't trust the staff. The headmaster was no better. Robert dreamed about being a military man. He wanted to join the Air Force. Getting as far away from Loudown was a driving force within him. Every night, before he slept, he would stare at the bottom of the bunk above him. He dreamt of faraway places; this, after a long night of studying. That was after intense football practice, which came after a long day in school. His days started at 0430 hours with hygiene, sometimes unreasonable chores, and breakfast. Robert was excellent at all he did. He didn't do it for any adult approval. He had been let down so many times by adults he learned to be self-reliant. He did it for himself. He did it for his chance to escape a pitiful childhood. Robert was driven. Even though he was a loner, he was discreet and smart enough to stay out of trouble. Because of his natural charisma, many boys gravitated toward him as their leader. However, he rejected their allegiance. Robert was focused on the future. He didn't let power plays and pride distract him.

There was one boy that Robert couldn't resist taking under his wing. Benjamin came to the home when Robert was fifteen. Benny was eight. He was autistic, scared, and shy. He was African American, which also made him a target for racial slurs.

One day, while Benny was fulfilling his chores of taking out the trash to the bin in the back alley, a thug and his four friends cornered Benny to make fun of him. They decided to take his nice shoes and choke him until he nearly passed out. Robert happened to be looking out the window of his room, which faced the alley. Robert heard the commotion but couldn't see what was going on. Normally, he stayed out of those confrontations; they were a frequent occurrence despite the staff, however, this time, Robert had a sinking feeling that Benny was involved. He opened the window and stuck his head out to get a clearer look. As soon as he saw what was happening, he leaped out to the ground about six feet below.

Robert landed a well-guided right cross on the side of the main thug's head. He was temporarily dazed and out of commission. Robert quickly wheeled around to thwart the other attackers. One boy was about to slash Robert with a broken bottle. Fortunately, he was able to catch the attacker's arm, which he brought crashing down against the high part of his knee. The crack sound startled the other boys. The attacker writhed on the ground yelling, holding his broken arm. The other three started backing away from Robert as they cursed.

The loud skirmish brought the sorriest, meanest staff member running out. Being a big bullish goon himself, he was planning on slamming someone. It appeared to him that Robert was the instigator, so Robert was the object of his furry. He moved quickly toward Robert, fists clenched, veins in his head bulging, and hateful wrath in his eyes. Robert made a split-second decision: There couldn't be any place worse than Loudown. He wheeled around with a spinning kick. He caught the staff flush in the ribs. He went to one knee holding his mid-section. Robert then kicked him in the side of the head with all his might. The goon was sprawled on the ground, motionless for a few minutes. Out cold. As the boys looked on in shock, Robert grabbed Benny and sprinted for the rooms. While they ran, Robert told Benny to pack his things as quickly as possible. Robert ran into his room and had his few belongings rolled up and tied in a couple of shirts in about three minutes. He dashed to Benny's room to help him finish. By now, there was a lot of confusion and yelling. People were trying to explain and hear what had just happened in the alley. Robert and Benny escaped out of Benny's window. They were around the block and long gone before the staff realized they'd ran away.

Many boys came through Loudown. Robert was very observant; he constantly listened. Even when it appeared he wasn't paying attention, or when he was focused on something else, he absorbed conversations and information around him. The Brickshire Methodist Boy's Home had a good reputation. The reasonable boys said of Brickshire: "The days were long and busy with chores, chapel, school, sports, music, etc.—but they taught us a lot, and were kind and fair." The ones who said negative things were the thugs who didn't care about progressing in life with integrity. Boys were constantly entered and exited from various orphanages, shuttled around.

Robert knew the general part of Brooklyn where Brickshire was located. He was resourceful enough to find it without any problems. Benny followed without doubt; he trusted Robert completely. Robert was extremely polite and respectful as he worked the chain in order to speak with the director. When he finally got an audience with Mrs. Reeter after a lengthy wait, Robert laid out his case before the sympathetic director. He started by saying, "Ma'am, we had to run away from Loudown in Queens." She winced upon hearing the name—Loudown. "A group a thugs, which the staff couldn't or wouldn't control, trapped Benny here in the alley. They were about to seriously injure him or maybe kill him." Robert was careful to choose his words in order to describe his young friend. "Benny learns and understands things differently from the rest of us." As Mrs. Reeter and Robert locked eyes, he knew she understood what he meant.

Mrs. Reeter sighed and said, "We're over-crowded now. We don't have room for two more. I'll do all I can to find—"

"Beg your pardon, Ma'am, I have other plans for myself. I'm only asking for my friend here. I give you my word, he's no trouble. He's unobtrusive." At this, a look of dread came on Benny's face.

"Unobtrusive," responded Mrs. Reeter with a slight grin and raised eye brows. "You have a nice vocabulary and articulation

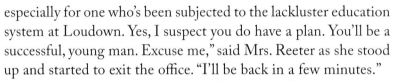

especially for one who's been subjected to the lackluster education system at Loudown. Yes, I suspect you do have a plan. You'll be a successful, young man. Excuse me," said Mrs. Reeter as she stood up and started to exit the office. "I'll be back in a few minutes."

"Uh… no… I—I—I want to stick with you. You're my—uh… my best friend. P-p-please?" stammered Benny as he started to cry.

Robert moved to the front of his chair and twisted so he could put both hands on Benny's shoulders. He looked intently into Benny's eyes and said, "I don't have a place to live yet. I'll be in school all day and work all evening for a while. Listen to me; this is a much better place for you."

Mrs. Reeter reentered. Robert sat back in his chair. She said, "Well, we can squeeze Benny into our humble home. We'd love to have him."

With that, Robert put his hand on Benny's arm and said, "I'll come and visit you when I can." Robert stood, thanked Mrs. Reeter, and departed into the unknown. Robert visited Benny three times, and then he never saw him again.

As Robert stepped out of the bedroom into the hallway, it disappeared. He was in the lobby of a luxurious hotel. He recognized it. It was the Le Meurice in Paris. There was a lot of activity. Men were moving around quickly. They were all wearing basic black suits, white shirts, and dark ties. Some were wearing small headsets, others speaking into walkie-talkies. He knew they were Secret Service agents.

When Robert looked to his left, there it was, about ten feet away: the prince of demons. He opened his hand, and revealed the diamond necklace that Robert bought for Audra for her birthday. With his composed manner restored, the demon said, "The next piece was going to be a beautiful engagement ring, but you blew it. Your slipping mental faculties, also known as old age, caused her death. Am I trying to deceive you? This, you merely believe—know deep down inside, true?" As Robert's head dropped, the demon knew he scored a point. The archfiend leapt on his wounded prey. "Robert, it's very doubtful you'll stop Muslov. Why live with two devastating failures? A lovely seaside villa here in France would be a wonderful place to get over Audra, and meet a delightful, voluptuous French woman."

It snapped its finger, and they were on the balcony of a spacious flat overlooking the Bay of Biscay. The breeze was perfectly warm, the sky a cloud-dotted, rich blue, and the caressing sun was at 1030 hours. The music of gently crashing waves from the emerald water, rustling leaves, and melodic birds soothed Robert's ears. Sitting in a chair in white linen, was a gorgeous, dark haired, dark eyed woman. *Yeah,* Robert thought, *It would be nice.* The demon was relentless and good at being evil.

Robert felt very tired. He staggered into the villa, looking for a bed. The demon was extremely pleased. Robert saw a very comfortable looking bed and couldn't get there soon enough. Four pillows with rich, soft light-brown material rested on a darker brown, perfectly worn comforter. The prince gently whispered, "Rest, my liege, rest." However, Robert's sense of duty kept pricking his mind. It was the most comfortable, warm bed he had ever laid on, but he couldn't get lost in sleep. His conscience kept nagging him. The prince sent a chilly breeze over Robert, trying to coax him to get under the covers. The demon, in a soft, soothing voice said, "Just for a few minutes until you get warm." For a second, Robert had a moment of clarity about who was talking to him. He sprang to his feet and staggered toward the door. "You fool!" cried the demon. "You'll never catch him being as tired as you are!" Joshua started to run. Good move.

As Robert ran, he noticed the trees and buildings had started to slowly transform. Before long, the trees were tall pines and oaks covered in Spanish moss. The buildings turned into old wood frame houses. The heat and humidity increased noticeably too. He walked on the right side of the crudely paved road. There were no sidewalks. He was drawn to a house on the left. It had a clean

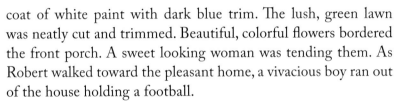

coat of white paint with dark blue trim. The lush, green lawn was neatly cut and trimmed. Beautiful, colorful flowers bordered the front porch. A sweet looking woman was tending them. As Robert walked toward the pleasant home, a vivacious boy ran out of the house holding a football.

As he sprang off the porch, he said, "I'm gonna play with Ronnie."

"I want you home at five thirty," responded the mother.

"Yes, Mamma." He ran past Robert and down the street. Robert smiled at his youthful energy.

As Robert soaked in this rare, pleasant moment, he didn't know he was about to get another uplifting surprise. He decided to walk into the house. After taking one step into the home, he was stopped dead in his tracks by the other person in the clean, modest, organized living room.

CHAPTER 13

MUSLOV'S JOURNEY

M uslov stood on the edge of a barren, gray cliff. As far as could be seen in either direction, there was no vegetation, not even a weed, nothing but gray dust and rock. The whole sky was equally dreary and overcast. On the ground, about twenty-five feet away from him, sat a disheveled, haggard, gaunt woman wearing a dirty, torn dress. She cried out in her native language, "No my son! Don't do this. Please!"

While never casting a glance toward her, in a calm voice, he commanded, "Remove her from my presence—for good." Two demons swooped down to take her away. His last command was, "Don't hurt her."

As he turned back toward the edge, two massive eye-shaped clearings appeared in the clouds. Instead of seeing blue sky, he beheld what Miles saw; he was looking at the world through Miles' eyes literally.

When Muslov first shot through the pulsating light, he landed in a dingy back alley at night. His subconscious dream world was darker and more faded than Robert's, Magnus's, and Mile's. He was immediately confronted with the horribly beaten body of his father. He never actually knew where his dad was pummeled, nor did he ever see his corpse; the funeral had been closed casket, and Mrs. Deshnue wouldn't allow her children to see the body. However, Muslov obsessively imagined what the whole scene looked like. In fact, the detailed scenarios he played over and over and over in his mind contributed greatly to his emotional and mental destruction. The mad genius wasn't surprised about being there. It was merely par for the course since he'd thought about it so much. As he started to turn and walk away, the head

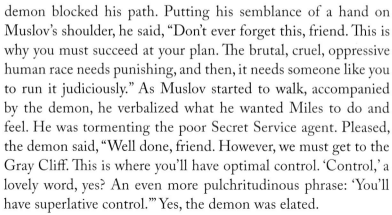

demon blocked his path. Putting his semblance of a hand on Muslov's shoulder, he said, "Don't ever forget this, friend. This is why you must succeed at your plan. The brutal, cruel, oppressive human race needs punishing, and then, it needs someone like you to run it judiciously." As Muslov started to walk, accompanied by the demon, he verbalized what he wanted Miles to do and feel. He was tormenting the poor Secret Service agent. Pleased, the demon said, "Well done, friend. However, we must get to the Gray Cliff. This is where you'll have optimal control. 'Control,' a lovely word, yes? An even more pulchritudinous phrase: 'You'll have superlative control.'" Yes, the demon was elated.

As they walked down the street of what appeared to be a God forsaken city, a fog appeared right in front of them. In the fog, as they got closer, Muslov saw a small, head-level window. When he peered through it, he was back in his apartment face to face with Robert. After a few minutes, he knew he was being interrogated. He said, "No one, no one can decode my years of master planning and work!"

The demon pulled him away from the window and said, "Let's go. Time management is crucial. Patience is not a virtue. Time is money, or in my—er, your case, both capital and power." Fortunately for the demon, Muslov was so preoccupied, he wasn't paying close attention.

"So, with your power," questioned Muslov, "Why can't you instantly transport me to the Gray Cliff? Of course, this 'Gray Cliff,' as you call it, is really the corpus callosum or ventricle of the brain." The demon was furious at Deshnue's audacity.

He grabbed Muslov by the throat, lifted him high off the ground, and brought Deshnue's face to within inches from his own hooded pseudo-face. The demon's breath smelled like death. With a low, growling voice, he said, "Listen to me you arrogant mother f***er. You won't accomplish s**t without me. Not a damn thing. Who do you think helped you conceive and contrive this plan? Who's going to help you execute it?" He put Muslov down, slightly bowed, and said, "Yours truly." With that, he turned and walked away, and then, he said in a pleasant voice, "Follow me."

They walked for what seemed a long time for Muslov. The city street they walked down was boring and nothing worth attention. Deshnue walked about five meters behind the prince. The archfiend stopped, with his back still toward Muslov. He remained silent, and he extended his left hand. He wanted Deshnue to behold something on that side. It was Deshnue's childhood home during happier days: beautiful flowers, full trees, and green grass. The house looked inviting. In the yard, Muslov observed himself as a child, playing with his two older sisters, younger brother, and the family dog. His eyes moistened. Without turning, the demon spoke, "Stay here awhile. Walk around. Reminisce on better times. Think about what this world stole from you. I need to attend to some business. I'll be back. Don't leave." Before he departed, he had one last comment. This time he turned to look at Muslov, "No more nonsense about this corpus callosum or ventricle. We must control Miles's heart." The prince vanished.

Muslov was torn on the inside. He didn't want to go in and see the pleasant memories, but he was compelled. It all came back to him: the stone walkway, the stone house that looked like a Thomas Kinkade painting, and the simple, but elegant, wooden front door. As a boy, the eight-by-eight-inch engraved, clouded glass on the door was too high for him to look through, and that was his standard of measurement. He always got excited when he thought he was getting taller or closer to being able to look through it. Now, of course, he could look through the window. He wasn't able to distinguish much on the inside. He put his hand on the helve, and left it there for several seconds. Did the demon mean *don't leave from the place where he left him standing outside the gate* or did he mean *don't leave this estate*? Besides, Muslov couldn't decide if he wanted to walk through the house anyway. He was completely distracted from his mission. Evil had made a mistake.

The internal struggle raged within him. Right or wrong, he opened the door and stepped inside, but there was no floor. As he fell, the air grew colder. He landed in a large snow drift. He hated Lazo, Siberia. His madness drove him there many years ago. At the time, he wanted the isolation. It was the ideal place to conceive his plan. It served its purpose. Still, he loathed it. It all came back to him: the bitter cold, the massive amounts of snow, and the loneliness. However, he also remembered, though fleeting, the pleasant seasons. Lazo had redeeming qualities, but alas, Muslov dropped in during one of the non-redemptive times. He wanted out of this dream sequence as soon as possible.

That's all he thought about: *getting out of here.* He was oblivious to what was around him. He didn't even notice the many imps swirling about him.

The small window in the fog, of which there are many, is the connection to the conscious, real world. There is a head demon and many imps, probably ushered in through humans, who are prompting evil and thwarting good. Control of the infiltrated person can be facilitated by verbalizing commands and demands; however, the most effective control comes from the Gray Cliff, the headquarters, the heart. This world is just like one's dreams: nonsensical at times, hazy, and very unpredictable. Even though one is not looking, and communicating through the window, he or she can still function in the material world, though they're almost like a zombie there; they don't function effectively. They're in somewhat of an inebriated state.

Robert stopped, put his hands on his hips and took a deep breath as he collected his thoughts.

Now, about the prince of darkness and his demons: they're always lurking, invisibly, in the world, searching for a receptive vessel. The most vulnerable are people filled with fear and hatred. The imps can effectively terrorize a poor soul. However, the situation with Muslov

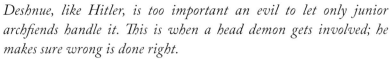

Deshnue, like Hitler, is too important an evil to let only junior archfiends handle it. This is when a head demon gets involved; he makes sure wrong is done right.

The heart of man is where activity begins, good or bad. It is a spiritual, intangible thing that can't be scientifically analyzed.

Will leaned back in the chair, rubbed his eyes, stretched, put his hands behind his head and thought out loud. "Dreams—do they give glimpses into one's future? Can they all be interpreted through the prism of basic sexuality, à la Sigmund Freud? Are they the result of anxieties, or are they the product of too much cold pizza before bedtime? What about the dreams most people have in common? Like being inadequately clothed in a public place and the sense of relief when waking and realizing it was a dream and not reality. Or, the one about falling and waking right before hitting the ground. There is the one of moving heavily, sluggishly. How about the thrilling sensation of being able to fly? And finally, there are nightmares, some too horrible and scary to recount. This is what the three adventurers are encountering. There are a lot of unknowns. There are a lot of uncontrollable factors."

―――――

Muslov finally noticed the imps. He screamed at them, "Get me out of here!" They swirled about and squealed in confusion. They weren't sure what to do. Why did he hate this memory so much? Was it the loneliness and seclusion, or was there a small part of him that loathed what he was doing? This place was where the grand plan was molded.

Suddenly, a huge grip latched onto the back of Muslov's neck, picked him up, and hurled him. As Deshnue was flying through the air, he heard the head archfiend's ominous voice, "Listen to me!" Muslov had never felt such fear. Not at all gently, the prince caught him and put Deshnue down on the ground in front of Muslov's childhood home in the exact spot where he left him. Muslov then understood; he was to stay in that very place. However, eventually, that would be impossible. One has no control of the wild ride on which dreams can take him or her. Deshnue heard the demon give up a grunting, growling noise, and it was off again. Muslov was so paralyzed with fear, he didn't even look around or shift his feet. He stood there, looking straight ahead with his hands to his side. He didn't know what to do. He was confused. Once again, evil made a mistake. Time was of the essence. Deshnue needed to maintain focus in order to carry out his diabolical plan. Evil has an unhealthy appetite for control. In the prince's lust for dominance in this scheme, he was hurting Muslov's ability to execute. Evil always, always, shoots itself in the foot. However, it can do tremendous damage before crippling itself.

Muslov didn't notice when it appeared, but the fog and window were immediately in front of him. The only problem: He would have to take two paces to look through it. *Can I move two steps?* He didn't want to further anger the demon. He decided he needed to check in with the real world. He was still on the couch in his apartment. However, the way Robert, Magnus, and the other agents were moving about and talking, he had a hunch things were about to change. Even though Deshnue was still confident that Will couldn't crack his system, he became nervous and agitated when he was grabbed and escorted to the makeshift lab. He snapped under the pressure. He started cursing, yelling, and putting up resistance to no avail.

Deshnue jerked back from the window. *I've got to get to the Gray Cliff,* he said to himself. *What's the delay? If this—whatever he is—is as good as he portrays himself to be, how come I'm not there already?* Now his anger was starting to overcome his fear.

He started to come back to himself. He decided it would be best to try and stay put. Even though he hated the prince and his imps, he deemed them useful. He knew there was an important thing he could do while he was waiting: Speak into Miles. "Remember, this is a large group of powerful racists. Ultimately, because of the color of your skin, you're nothing to them. They hate you. They think you're subhuman. Get them before they get you. Make them pay."

Not quite good enough. The goodness of Miles, his sense of duty, was able to banter effectively with that hateful voice inside of him.

So what if they're racists? Regardless of whether I hate them or not, I won't ruin my life by doing something stupid. Still, he was starting to loathe these leaders. Muslov had more time to work on the young Secret Service agent.

In a gravely, hideous voice, an imp hovered close to Deshnue and said, "You don't have him yet—not completely."

Muslov pondered this for a few minutes, then spoke into Miles again, "You understand human nature. This G8 Summit is merely a dog and pony show. The question is which leader has the most diabolical ulterior motive? Which one will decide he has the edge, the ability to make the first move—the first strike for total world dominance, to solidify his or her own fame, fortune, and power? Let's face it, that's the supreme goal for man." Deshnue's hypocrisy is incredible. However, he'll resort to whatever he thinks it will take to totally win over Miles.

Mistrust was growing in Miles. He was even losing confidence in the President of the United States. He was starting to feel like he couldn't trust anyone. *Hm, sure, I'd spend the rest of my life in a super max in Colorado, I might be executed, but in the long run, would I be helping humanity, saving lives?* Now Deshnue had him seriously thinking. If he could get to the Gray Cliff in time, Miles would be forever trapped in the web.

The scene Muslov was in immediately changed. He was naked and standing in the middle of a busy office at Dynomated World Wide. He was ashamed and anxious to get out of there. However, everywhere he went, there were many coworkers and total humiliation. He felt relief when he realized a couple of archfiends picked him up and whisked him away. Within seconds, he was fully clothed again and standing at the edge of a cliff in a gray,

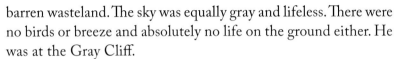

barren wasteland. The sky was equally gray and lifeless. There were no birds or breeze and absolutely no life on the ground either. He was at the Gray Cliff.

"Well done," the voice of the head demon came from behind Muslov. Deshnue wheeled in fear.

Was the prince being sarcastic? Muslov thought he'd seriously messed up by not staying put at his childhood home, but then he realized he didn't have any control over the situation. He was confused. Would the prince be angry even if it wasn't his fault?

Since Muslov was visibly shaken, the demon assured him, "Relax my friend. Those things that you spoke into Mr. Williams were well done. Yes, I'm pleased, excellent prep work. Now that you're at the Gray Cliff, the darkness of his heart, the deed will be done."

CHAPTER 14
ROBERT'S SURPRISE

The modest home was decorated and touched with love. The pictures of well groomed, dressed up children adorned the walls. A picture of dignified parents graced the parapet as well. However, Robert didn't notice. He could barely contain his excitement and relief when he uttered the name Magnus. Magnus was less able to contain himself when he gave Robert a man hug.

Robert hardly noticed the little girl, thinking she was somehow a part of the dream scene. She smiled at Robert and said, "Hi, I'm Nadia!" Robert looked a bit puzzled and startled.

Magnus quickly interjected, "She's the woman's daughter in the... tragic Sarajevo mission. I need to keep her with me in order to prevent the demons from getting her."

Robert was concerned that she would be a distraction. However, he wasn't sure what to say so he didn't comment. In this dream world, who knew what was right or wrong? No one had ever explored this realm before. Still standing in the living room, Robert said, "Let's compare mental notes. We have demons with a master who is trying to detour us. Using our pasts seems to be his weapon of choice. Air Force One is a factor, and I believe it all has something to do with the G8 Summit in Paris."

"And what about the African American gentleman and this home?" questioned Magnus. He observed that the diplomas and pictures on the wall of one particular young man played a part in all of this. There was a college diploma recognizing a degree in Education from the University of Southern Alabama. Above it, the picture of a handsome young man dressed in a policeman's uniform. Next to that, a picture of the same person, though a little older, wearing a crisp, dark, professional suit and tie. Below

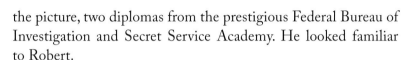

the picture, two diplomas from the prestigious Federal Bureau of Investigation and Secret Service Academy. He looked familiar to Robert.

"Yes," said Robert in a hushed tone as if he received a major revelation, a moment of enlightenment. "We need to accomplish two things. First, we need to find the window. We must put the team to work fast. Let's go. We'll talk about this on the move; time is of the essence. The director needs to get the African American Secret Service agent, or agents, working at the G8 Summit pulled off the mission. It may be too late for that, however. Second, we need to find Muslov."

Robert gave a long glance at Nadia. Magnus noticed, and he immediately said, "She won't be a hindrance."

Already, she couldn't keep pace. Magnus picked her up and carried her.

"Joshua," started Robert in an authoritative, yet fatherly tone, "She's not real. This is a dream world." Robert stopped and then spoke again. "I have an idea. Let's leave her with this family. I can tell they're good, responsible, God-fearing people. Hurry and take her back there before this scene changes."

Magnus understood this was a command. He didn't hesitate. He quickly carried her inside and put her on the couch. As he walked out of the door, he turned and made eye contact with her and said, "Don't leave this house, you'll be okay—I'll be okay."

Through a sniffle and tears she said, "Okay."

As Magnus jogged off the porch and toward Robert, he locked eyes with the matriarch. With a warm light in her gaze, she gave him a confident, encouraging sweet grin and said, "Them demons ain't gonna mess with a prayin' momma." Magnus felt assured.

No sooner did Magnus catch up with Robert when the scene changed. They could barely see. It appeared to be a gently descending tunnel. It wasn't man-made, but a natural passage bored through gray rock. While Robert was questioning whether they should go back or continue forward, which meant down,

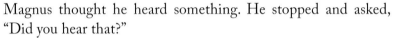

Magnus thought he heard something. He stopped and asked, "Did you hear that?"

"No. What do you think you heard?"

"It sounded like metal against metal."

They stood there for about ten seconds in silence but didn't hear anything. They continued down the gentle slope. After a few minutes—rattle, clank, rattle—this time Robert heard the faint sound too.

"It's getting louder," observed Magnus.

"Somehow, I think down is getting us closer to Deshnue," said Robert.

"I have a feeling the further down we go in the tunnel, the further we get from the window to the conscious world," observed Magnus. Robert was impressed with this insight but troubled by the probable truth. This would mean that the only option to stop this diabolical plan was to catch Muslov in this crazy, unpredictable, surreal world. *Whose soul were they going deeper into? Was it Muslov's, one of their own, or a combination of all three?* They now heard the louder, distinct sound of chains rattling.

CHAPTER 15

CLOSING IN

"The deeper we get into evil, the further we drift from reality, common sense, peace, goodness, and most of all, the conscious world," guessed Magnus.

"I think it's just you and me young man," said Robert too soon. They were both startled by the rattling chains because they were right next to the source of the sound. It came from a cleft in the side of the tunnel. They both stood still, staring at the opening.

"Come to the entrance. Show yourself," commanded Robert coolly.

There was silence for a few seconds, and then—shuffle, rattle, boyish groan, shuffle, rattle, boyish groan. Bound in chains, a skinny boy of approximately ten years of age appeared at the opening. He was obviously scared. He shielded his eyes from what little light was in the tunnel. Magnus moved around to get a better angle on seeing the boy's face. It was vaguely familiar.

Robert had a hunch that this tunnel, with its downward slope, would lead them to Deshnue. They both felt this imprisoned little boy could offer clues to his location.

The little boy curled up the best he could, despite being hindered by the chains and shackles, on the ground at the entrance of the opening. He tried to hide his face. Both Robert and Magnus knelt down to be less intimidating to the pathetic being. Robert lightly touched his head and asked, "Do you know Muslov Deshnue, son?"

In a sad, soft voice, he responded, "Y-yes. I-I'm Muslov Deshnue." Robert and Magnus looked at one another in wonder. "I-I'm a g-g-good boy—really." They both felt deep pity for Muslov.

Evil preys on vulnerability. A brilliant young man, touched directly by horrible tragedy, was a perfect target for the wicked one. It was a perfect storm, if you will. A righteous anger rose up in a mighty tempest within Robert as he looked at the helpless, young Muslov. That indignation drove him to yell at the chains, "Release this child!" To the amazement of Magnus and the frightened little boy, the chains and shackles crumbled to dust. The lad was free. In another deep recess of this subconscious world, the head demon recoiled with fear. The imps were confused and scared.

Robert and Magnus gently tried to help the frail boy to his feet. He looked similar to a baby colt trying to stand for the first time. "If he can even walk, it'll be very labored and slow," observed Magnus.

"We'll take turns carrying him on our backs," concluded Robert. Without hesitation, Magnus knelt down, and Robert helped secure the boy on Magnus piggy-back style.

Robert gently placed his hand on young Muslov's back and asked, "How do we find the older you?" Before the boy could speak, there was a brilliant flash of light, and the scene changed. The boy clung tighter to Magnus. He was gripped with fear. How many years had he been shackled in that tunnel? How long has it been since he has only seen gray walls?

They were back in the yard of Muslov's childhood home. Young Muslov's grip on Magnus loosened, and his expression became more pleasant. Based on the boy's reaction, it didn't take Robert long to figure out where they were. Deshnue often thought about his favorite place. Magnus sat him down on a grassy, lush area, in the shade under a full elm-like tree. The boy looked happy. Robert said to Magnus, "We need a little rest. Lie down here for about an hour. I'll stay awake first, then we'll switch, assuming the setting doesn't change." Magnus gladly nodded and didn't hesitate to curl up under the tree. He was asleep in no time.

The little boy was in such an obvious place of peace as he gazed around the yard. Robert hesitated to disturb him, but he

needed some information. "What do you know about the plan? How can we stop it?"

It appeared that the boy was not paying attention. However, after eight seconds, he said, "If I can stay here, I'll tell you all you need to know."

Without knowing what young Muslov knew, Robert was hesitant to agree. Though, what alternative did he have? "If you tell us everything, we'll leave you here."

With a boyish grin, Muslov quickly replied, "Okay!" He didn't waste any time. "The tunnel where you found me will take you to the Gray Cliff. That's where you want to go. That's where you'll find—" The boy froze with horror on his face. Robert turned to look where Muslov was staring. In the distance, was the unmistakable form of the head demon. A rage for the evil presence welled within Robert to an uncontrollable peak. He stormed toward the archfiend. It was a mistake. Not that the demon was going to confront the fearless Joshua, but he was drifting too far from young Muslov and Magnus. This wasn't the prince's plan; he only wanted to intimidate the little boy so that he wouldn't talk. However, it had the unexpected effect of leading Robert away from where he should have been.

The demon fled. When Robert turned back toward the yard, it wasn't there. He was in a city alley. It was night. There were three police officers beating a man. It didn't take Robert long to realize this was Boris Deshnue. After the so-called policemen left, Robert felt pity for Muslov and hoped he had not viewed this scene. Robert knelt down and tried to comfort Boris. With one last, weak gasp, he muttered. Robert was good at Romanian, but Boris was hard to understand. He did provide vital information, however. "Go back to our house. Go in—tunnel to the Gray Cliff. Love Muslov—good boy…"

"Okay, how do I get back to the house," a frustrated Robert asked. He was tired beyond tired. He was talking to himself. He was the only living being in the alley. He sat with his back against the wall. His head started bobbing. He leaned it back against the bricks. As soon as he fell into a deeper sleep, his head fell, which roused him awake. He couldn't think straight. Crazy thoughts were swirling in his mind.

Suddenly, an image appeared that gave him renewed hope. Mrs. Reeter was standing next to Benny, holding his hand. Neither had aged. Benny was bouncing up and down with excitement, pointing down the street. Mrs. Reeter, in her calm, dignified manner, said, "Follow us." She led Benny and started walking down the alley.

Robert drifted and stumbled behind them. He didn't notice anything around him. In fact, there was nothing around him. He was in a hazy, gray void. He focused on Mrs. Reeter's back. Benny occasionally turned and excitedly exhorted Robert, "Come on!"

At times, Joshua wasn't sure he could continue. He continually whispered, "Help me God." Between the prayers and the sight of Mrs. Reeter and Benny, he would make it.

About ten minutes later, though it seemed much longer to Robert, they were back in the yard of Muslov's childhood home. Mrs. Reeter took Robert by the arm and led him to a tree. Sitting in the shade was Audra. "Rest awhile," said Mrs. Reeter. Robert curled up and leaned against Audra's breast. The last thing he remembered before he drifted to sleep was Audra's arm embracing him and the soft touch of her hand. He felt comforted and hopeful.

Waking was a great labor for Robert. When he realized Audra was rousing him, he felt renewed courage, hope, and strength. He stared into Audra's gentle, loving eyes. He squinted and rubbed them until he could focus clearly. He made it to his feet and stood tall. He took Audra by the hand and helped her stand. He didn't want to stop looking into her eyes, but he knew it was time to move on. When he looked at Mrs. Reeter, she said, "You and Magnus must go into the house. Then, go into the hallway

closet. This will lead you into the tunnel and, ultimately, to the Gray Cliff."

He looked around until he spotted Magnus. He, young Muslov, and an elderly woman he didn't recognize were under the tree where he left the two guys. They were sitting with their heads bowed. The elderly woman was speaking; the other two were silent. It appeared she was praying. After a few minutes, the three finished and stood. They walked over and joined the other four. Magnus proudly introduced his grandmother to the rest of the group. With equal pride, Robert introduced Mrs. Reeter, Benny, and Audra. Robert turned, and stood face to face with Audra. He didn't want to leave, but he knew he must. Mrs. Reeter stepped toward him, put her hand gently on his shoulder, and said, "Leave her and young Muslov with us. She'll be okay. Evil doesn't dare mess with a praying grandmother and an orphanage home mother."

Robert kissed Audra's hand, looked at Magnus, and said, "Let's go."

Dorcus instructed them. "When you walk through the front door. You'll have an unmistakable sign for which door is the closest that will take you through the tunnel and, ultimately, the Gray Cliff."

Magnus had a slightly perplexed look on his face and started, "What sign are—"

"You'll know," interrupted Dorcus with a reassuring smile. Without making eye contact with anyone, Robert turned and started his determined walk toward the front door. Magnus followed, but stopped briefly to look back at his grandmother. She gave him an encouraging nod. He also couldn't help giving young Muslov a quick glance. His hatred of evil intensified.

They were both struggling to focus. The emotions of being with loved ones and the exhaustion were overwhelming, but focus they must. They knew it; they had no other choice. They stepped into the beautiful old home. The well-preserved wooden floors, exquisite woodwork around the doors and windows, and freshly painted walls made the house very warm and inviting. Magnus didn't notice. The first thing that caught his eye was an antique, life-sized doll sitting in a wooden chair in the entrance way. Her hand was raised so that it pointed at a door. Magnus chuckled and shook his head. He recognized the doll. "She's pointing toward the door we need to go through," said Magnus with a smile. It was obvious this mannequin brought back many memories for Stone.

With a grin, Robert said, "I want to hear this story sometime." He immediately opened the door and stepped through. Magnus followed. Again, in the dark, they were freefalling.

CHAPTER 16

THE LAST STAND

As before, they alighted on the ground. They were in the tunnel. There was nothing but cold, gray rock all around them. Once again, without speaking, they started walking the gentle downward slope. Suddenly, after about ten minutes, Robert stopped and asked, "Did you hear that?" Magnus nodded. It was the faint sound of someone shouting.

As they got closer to the source, it was the unmistakable shouts of cursing and threats: "Go back, Mother F***er! I'll kill your b***h a**! Stay the f**k out of here. My house! My f***ing house! I'm gonna kill ya!" Robert and Magnus didn't slow down. They had come too far emotionally, mentally, and physically to be intimidated. They saw the dark shape of the man as they approached. When they were upon him, they beheld the most pitiful homeless looking human being imaginable. His clothes were filthy, torn rags, their colors couldn't even be determined. They were all dark, greasy, and sooty. The man's skin looked similar and clung to his bones. He was extremely gaunt. His hair looked like a bush. Magnus and Robert could never recognize him as the person they saw in one of the pictures at Miles's childhood home. "I guard this f***ing fork, Mother F***er! No passes! I kill damn it! F*** you. I'm Marcus!" The bravado coming from such a shell of a man was almost comical. Robert and Magnus didn't notice it until Marcus said it: They had indeed come to a fork in the tunnel.

Robert was in no mood. He grabbed the skinny Marcus by the neck and shoved him against the wall. With a deep, growling, determined voice, Joshua commanded, "No games. Which way do we go? Where is Muslov Deshnue?"

Marcus began to beg and cry. When Robert released him, he fell to the ground. "They'll kill me. Please don't let them kill me. Please go back. I don't need no mo' trouble." He began to whimper.

This time Magnus was the gentle "good cop." He knelt down to the pathetic shell of a man, put his hand on his shoulder, and in a calm tone said, "We don't want to bring you any trouble. Please tell us which tunnel to use, and we'll leave you alone."

"They won't leave me alone," responded Marcus as he looked up the tunnel, wiping the tears from his eyes. A few archfiends were lurking there.

Magnus profoundly questioned Marcus. "Look at you man. What else can they do to you?"

"Miles always did the right thing. He's a good man. I don't want nothin' to happen to 'im. Yah, f**k it. I guess they can't do mo' to me," responded Marcus reflectively.

"Here's the key, my man," advised Magnus, "Don't let them scare you. Fear is their main weapon."

With a chuckle, Robert interjected, "He doesn't have to tell us anything." He nodded toward the fork. The same doll that pointed them to the right door for the tunnel was propped against the wall. She was pointing to the left path. A pleasant light was shining on her. There was some kind of bundle on the ground next to the doll. Robert went to check it. It was a thick knit forest green blanket. Robert was moved when he picked it up and held it. He obviously recognized it, and that blanket meant a lot to him.

He brought the blanket and doll to Marcus. Robert handed the afghan to him, and propped the doll up against the nearest wall. Marcus was almost in shock. He wrapped himself in the blanket. For the first time in a very, very long while, he had a content, pleasant look on his face. He said, "I forgot how good it feels to be warm. I've been cold for so long." He looked over at the doll and said, "Hello, my name is—is Marcus. Can we be friends?" They left Marcus with a peaceful look on his face.

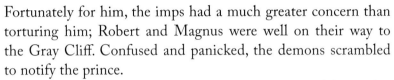

Fortunately for him, the imps had a much greater concern than torturing him; Robert and Magnus were well on their way to the Gray Cliff. Confused and panicked, the demons scrambled to notify the prince.

Robert and Magnus started the slow descent. After a few minutes of silence, Magnus asked, "May I ask what the story is behind the blanket?"

After about ten seconds, Robert spoke. "I never knew my… parents, if that's what you can call them. I lived in a few orphanages. There was very little stability in my life except for one thing. There was a janitor at a particular home. I lived at this one from the ages of three to eight. His name was Hank. Shortly after I got there, he gave me that blanket. I later found out that his wife made it. It's been the most warm and comforting thing I've ever had." After a far away, sad look, Robert continued, "When I was a teenager, Benny and I had to make a quick get away from a dump in Queens called Loudown… I can't believe I left it there. I forgot it." Magnus sensed Robert was lost in quiet reflection so he didn't speak. Moments later, Joshua again shared. "Hank was a great man, though few people knew it. He was a humble, unassuming person. He was like the poor widow that Jesus talked about in the Bible." Magnus was surprised. He didn't know Robert was a man of the Word. "On the day I left that home, Hank gave me a Bible and told me to be a man like Jesus. I still have that sacred text." After a brief pause, Robert continued, "I'm a prodigal son. Maybe it's time for me to come back home to the Father." Robert believed that the farther they went down the tunnel, the farther away they moved from the land of the living. He kept this thought to himself. He desperately hoped and prayed that Magnus would make it back to his family. Personally, he was prepared for the end.

Seventy-five yards ahead, they saw what looked like an opening. When they got thirty yards away, it was, in fact, a clearly defined passage. They stepped through to a dark, gray hazy world.

The two massive eye-shaped openings in the clouds grabbed their attention. They were glued to the scene. Many smartly dressed people were walking around in a spacious conference room; news crews, reporters, Secret Service agents, and French Police officers were present. George W. Bush, Condoleezza Rice, Dmitry Medvedev, and Hu Jintao were clearly visible. Robert and Magnus heard a voice barking orders. It came from Muslov standing at the edge of a cliff—the Gray Cliff. "Now's the time, Miles. Shoot Medvedev and Jintao!" The prince was hovering slightly over the Abyss, encouraging Deshnue.

Robert quickly dropped to one knee and bowed his head. He appeared to be praying. In fact, the prodigal son was coming back home to the Father. Robert jumped up and shouted toward Magnus, "You get Muslov!" Robert started running toward the cliff in the direction of where the head demon was hovering. Magnus ran to Deshnue. He was taking off his outer shirt at the same time. Before Muslov could react, Magnus had him on the ground, and was tying the shirt around his head, gagging Muslov's mouth. He easily had Deshnue pinned to the ground and silent. When Magnus looked to see what Robert was doing, he was about to get one of the greatest shocks of his life. With a stern look of determination, Robert was sprinting toward the prince. When he got to the edge of the cliff, he dove into the mid-section of the head demon. A hideous shriek of fear bellowed from the archfiend. Robert disappeared. The demon could no longer suspend in midair. He fell into the abyss. The horrible scream faded. There was a brief period of murmuring and confusion. What happened to Magnus's friend and mentor? What happened to Muslov's leader? What happened to the demons' parent?

Miles Williams had a dizzy spell, and his knees buckled. With all the activity, no one around him noticed. He was able to quickly

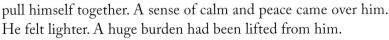

pull himself together. A sense of calm and peace came over him. He felt lighter. A huge burden had been lifted from him.

Meawhile, back in Deshnue's lab, the situation was much less calm. Robert flat-lined. The medic tried to revive him. They performed cardiopulmonary resuscitation and utilized the defibrillator for several minutes. It was no use. Robert Steele was dead.

Magnus ordered Deshnue to remove his shirt and pants. The lost genius foolishly tried to run. With little effort, Magnus caught him; he shoved him and sent him sprawling to the ground. Magnus removed, with force, the pitiful man's clothes. Deshnue was down to his plaid boxers. Magnus warned him, "I'm tired beyond belief, cold, hungry, thirsty, and worst of all, I just witnessed a friend die because of your sorry, demented a**. I want to kill you; I really want to kill you. Get us to the passage back to the other side." Magnus used the shirt to bind Muslov's hands behind his back and the pants to make a make shift leash that he put around Deshnue's neck. Stone started walking away from the cliff, jerking Muslov along. As they walked, the sad, hideous whimpers and cries from the demons faded. Magnus removed the gag from Muslov, and asked, "How do I get back?"

"I don't know." Magnus gave a hard jerk, Muslov groaned, "I—I really don't know. Please. I don't know." In fact, he didn't.

Magnus looked around, and in frustration yelled, "Where's that damn tunnel?!" After a few seconds, he regained his composure and whispered, "Dear God, please get me out of here." All that could be seen was gray ground and gray sky.

CHAPTER 17
LONGING FOR HOME

After a few minutes of walking, Magnus stopped. He thought out loud, "We should be going up, or at least remaining on the same level, not going down."

In a weak voice, Muslov said, "I think you're right."

Magnus surveyed the scene. He saw a slight upward slope so they started walking up the hill. Magnus couldn't get thoughts of Robert and his end out of his head. *Please, God, don't let him suffer*, was his silent prayer. Time was becoming crucial. Back at the lab, the medic was concerned about Magnus's vital signs. Fortunately, there was something different on the horizon. When they got close enough, Magnus felt renewed hope when he saw an unmistakable cave. Magnus didn't hesitate to go in, leading the stumbling Deshnue. It was the tunnel. Magnus felt encouraged.

After five minutes of walking through the tunnel, they came to the fork. Magnus was heartened when he saw Marcus curled up in peaceful sleep. Marcus was wrapped in Robert's blanket, even his head; only Marcus's face was visible. He was in the same spot Robert and Magnus had left him. The doll was in the same position next to his head. The sight of Marcus lost in sleep and warm, and memories of the mannequin, strengthened Magnus. He kept moving. Deshnue was seriously struggling to keep pace. Now, not only was he stumbling, but he was falling. Magnus untied Muslov's hands. Deshnue was no threat.

Just when Magnus was having doubts he would get back, just when he was praying for Andrea and Dawn's wellbeing, they started elevating. He and Deshnue were flying! Magnus recognized the landscape they were gliding over; it was the lush, rocky, wildflower-spotted Texas Hill Country. Then they were over an ocean, and before they knew it they were on solid ground. They were amongst a crowd on a city street. There was much hustle and bustle. Magnus was embarrassed when he realized he was naked. He grabbed Muslov and ducked behind a corner. He was relieved when he remembered it was only a dream world, and no one seemed to notice anyway. After the relief came anger. Magnus was fed up with this subconscious prison. Despair was setting in. Just then, Andrea walked by holding Dawn. What a boost! Andrea didn't stop. As she passed by, she looked over, smiled, and said, "Always walk toward the sun." Just before they got lost in the crowd, little Dawn, looking over her mother's shoulder, waved at him.

Magnus grabbed Muslov and said, "Let's go." With new energy and resolve, Magnus started chasing the sun and thankfully he was clothed again. Magnus recognized the bustling downtown of San Antonio, Texas. He felt better closer to home. The day was clear and crisp, not too crisp though; it was just right. However, after five minutes of walking, a thick fog started rolling in. Moments later, the window appeared. Magnus stopped to check in with the "real world." "Hey dudes," heard the startled agents from a weary Magnus. "How long have we been in this alternate universe?"

Will checked his watch and said, "Thirty-seven hours, Forty four minutes, and roughly twenty seconds."

"What's the news at the G8 Summit," wondered Magnus.

The agent who was monitoring it said, "So far so good. There have been no reports of any problems." With a pause, the same agent mustered his courage and said, "Mr. Steele—Robert is… dead."

"I know," the new Joshua responded solemnly. Magnus then questioned Will, "Any idea how I get back to Sarajevo? That's where I entered through the pulsating light." Will had a blank stare. The agents looked at him with concern. Magnus then told Will: "Get some rest."

Magus backed out of the window and moved-out. They continued walking. The fog cleared, and they were back in front of Muslov's childhood home. Under his breath, Magnus muttered, "I'm getting tired of this place." However, Muslov seemed to get a dose of renewed energy.

Muslov said, "My portal is in the backyard. I believe we can both get back through it." Deshnue was cooperating? Could he be trusted? Did he believe it was over? These questions swirled in Magnus's mind. Just then, as clear as can be, Magnus saw Robert looking out of one of the second floor windows. He had a glowing, almost angelic look on his face. It made Magnus feel very good. Robert gave Magnus an affirming nod. Magnus grabbed Muslov, went to the back of the house, and plunged head first into the pulsating light circle.

CHAPTER 18

HONORING ROBERT STEELE

The trip back was much rougher than the trip there. Magnus passed out. When he came to, he distinctly heard someone say, 'Clear,' and then a thud. When the cobwebs cleared from his mind, he realized he was in Deshnue's makeshift lab; and the agents were frantically trying to resuscitate Muslov. Moments later, after another attempt with the defibrillator, Muslov let out a gasp. He was alive again.

Magnus, still groggy in the chair, was given a bottle of water and an apple. It was the best water he ever tasted and the best apple he ever ate. They were real. The chair he was in was real. It was soaked with sweat, real sweat. He was back in the tangible world. "Mr. Smith. It's now 2017 hours. The director wants us to leave at 2030 hours. We'll go straight to the hospital to get you checked-out."

"Where is Robert?" asked Magnus.

"Allow me to show you." An agent took Magnus by the arm and helped him out of the chair. He led Magnus to the back porch. There was a large duffle bag neatly on the concrete slab. It was Robert's body. The agent was anxious to explain that the cool slab and crisp outside air was the best way to preserve his corpse. Magnus dropped his head and slowly walked back to the couch. He sat down and put his head back. As he drifted to sleep, good thoughts of Andrea, Dawn, and Robert floated in his mind.

Magnus was aroused awake. "Time to go… Mr. Stone," said one of the agents with slight indignation in his voice. Magnus didn't hear the agents load the van. Magnus was the last. Eventually, he would be the first. The outside air was refreshing. The van was cramped. Robert's body was laid on a whole seat.

His body bag was securely seat-belted. Robert's corpse, rightfully so, was treated with the utmost respect. He was an extremely precious cargo.

The other extra passenger was Muslov Deshnue. His hands were bound though it probably wasn't necessary. He was very weak and in serious condition. They needed to get him to the hospital quickly. The ride to the infirmary was a blur to Magnus. He slept almost the entire time while in the hospital. A couple of days later, at o-dark-thirty in the morning, he was subjected to a thorough physical and psychological examination. He was growing impatient. He couldn't wait to hug his wife and daughter.

Finally, he was released. It was 1622 hours. He didn't call Andrea. He wanted to surprise them. The reunion was not a disappointment. When he walked in the house, Andrea and Dawn were curled up on the couch. Andrea heard him enter. When she realized it was Magnus, with tears in her eyes, she gracefully got to her feet and poured her intense love for her husband through her hug. When Dawn was awake enough, and realized what was happening, she excitedly proclaimed, "Daddy!" Magnus got a lump in his throat when he heard that wonderful word.

For the next three days, Magnus rested and made the most of his time with his family. Then, the three were flown to Dulles Airport in order to attend Robert's funeral. Andrea asked no questions, and Magnus didn't talk about the mission until the day of the memorial service. As he fumbled with his tie, he simply said, "Robert made his peace with God before he… perished." Andrea walked over and gave her husband an encouraging touch on the arm.

Fittingly, the day of Robert's funeral was pleasant. It was brisk, but it felt good with the right warm clothing, and there was not a cloud in the sky. There were fifty-seven people in attendance. It all took place at the cemetery. It started promptly at 0930 hours. The director began: "I won't go over all of Robert's accolades he accumulated during his twenty-seven years of service to the UTD, his country, and the world. A few times, he has possibly saved the world from the brink of destruction. The world will never know. Even though I consider him a close friend, confidant, and comrade," the director said with a slightly choked and shaky voice, "I don't know much about his personal life, other than he never knew his parents. He was an orphan." Magnus sighed at this. He felt extremely privileged that Robert shared intimate childhood memories with him. Andrea tightened her grip on her husband's hand. This makes Robert even more of an inspiration. "He was an amazing professional. He always arrived early, and was impeccably dressed. This was indicative of his preparation for a mission. He thoroughly studied the information prior to beginning. He even did extra research on his own. He was the consummate agent. Robert, you made us all better. You've made the world better. We will strive to follow your example. Your legacy will live on. God bless and rest your soul."

After a moving rendition of Amazing Grace from a Scottish bagpiper and an inspirational prayer from a CIA Chaplain the service was over. Magnus sat for a few minutes, staring straight ahead. Andrea continued to hold her husband's hand in silence. The director walked over and sat next to Magnus. He joined Joshua in staring mutely. After a couple of minutes, he placed his hand on Magnus's shoulder and stood up and said, "I'll see you in exactly 30 days at 0730, lad." Without looking up at the director, Magnus responded, "0700, Sir."

PART II

MAKING OF MAGNUS

CHAPTER 19
THE BEEMER

Magnus laid in bed on his back, with Andrea's head on his chest, they were both wide awake. Magnus was feeling nostalgic. He said, "It appears our life together is destined to be an adventure."

With a smile, Andrea responded, "I think you're right, especially in light of our first few years together…"

At a construction site in downtown Austin, Texas, a nineteen year old young man was working hard cleaning up scraps. His supervisor really liked him. He was always on time and worked very hard. This laborer was extremely dependable. The employee's name was Magnus Stone. During lunch one day, Magnus was eating with his favorite co-laborer—a middle aged gentleman named Burnell. He was a Godly man with a lot of simple, profound wisdom. Magnus determined he got it from a rough past, however, Burnell didn't volunteer much about his former years. Burnell was married with two children and five grandchildren. He looked somewhat like the actor Samuel L. Jackson. In many ways, he became Magnus's mentor. On this particular day, they were eating lunch at their favorite spot: A shaded area on the second floor of the building they were helping to construct. They were across the street from a historic Lutheran church. In time, they observed that this sanctuary provided extensive services for the poor; many down trodden came in and out of a particular side door. A sign over the ingress read:

The foxes have holes, and the birds of the air have nests; but the son of man hath not where to lay his head–Matthew 8:20

For the first time, Magnus realized he had seen the same two-door, subdued red, BMW 740iL parked in front of the church on a regular bases. It caught his eye because such a nice car seemed out of place there. He was curious. This day would forever change his life. Toward the end of the shift, he happened to be laboring on the first floor of the construction site directly across the street from the Beemer, and the most beautiful girl he ever saw was fumbling with her keys, unlocking the door, and entering the driver's side. He was head over heels. The next day at lunch, he shared his feelings with Burnell.

While they sat eating lunch at their spot, Magnus said, "I'm in love, man. See the red BMW? That's the girl I want to spend the rest of my life with. How do I meet her?"

With a wry grin, Burnell joked, "You'll have to get a big bed to fit both you and the car. How do you know it's a she?"

"You know what I mean."

A little more serious—just a little—Burnell said, "She might be privileged. That's probably not a poor person's car. Here are some questions if she's well to do: Why is she working at the church? Is she working with the homeless and poor? Admirable. However, is she a prima donna? Maybe she's a wild girl who got into trouble and has to do community service … Probably not, I'll bet she's a nice young lady.

Now, back to your original question. Two approaches come to mind. First, put a rose on her windshield and follow it up with a poem. Then, invite her, through a note, to meet you at a coffee shop. Don't get your expectations too high, though. Second, you could start attending or volunteering there, but I like this option least. Don't use God and the church like that. If you intend to help, your motives should be right."

That night after dinner, sitting in a modest, small, yet clean and cozy living room, Magnus finally got the nerve up to breech the subject of "her" with his angelic, wise grandmother. He started, "I'm in love, Grandma."

As Dorcus rocked in her chair listening to J. Vernon McGee on the radio, she didn't respond. However, a slow grin slowly became visible on her face. Her silence didn't disconcert the lovesick young man. He knew his grandmother was processing. She would answer at the right time. When she spoke, she asked, "When you're not in love with her, will you still love her?" This was an odd inquiry to Magnus. He was convinced this feeling would last forever. Dorcus continued, "What if her face was horribly burned? What if she lost a breast to cancer?" Magnus was very confused about this line of questioning. She concluded, "What I'm getting at, my love, is do you know her? Do you know what's in her heart? Is she beautiful on the inside and not just the outside?"

Okay. Despite the confusion from his grandmother's words, it was finally settled in his adolescent, yet mature mind as he lay in bed, staring at the ceiling. *I'll put Burnell's plan into action and try to meet her.* As soon as the relief came from that resolution, the nervousness set in of how she'll react. He didn't get much sleep that night.

The next day at lunch, instead of going to their favorite spot to eat, Magnus took off down the street. As Burnell ate by himself, he wondered about the lad. About fifteen minutes later he saw Magnus walking up the street with a rose in his hand. Burnell smiled. He laughed when he observed Magnus nervously fumble with the windshield wiper blade and the flower. In an attempt to make a quick getaway, Magnus walked in front of an oncoming car. Fortunately, the auto wasn't going fast and quickly stopped. The irritated driver blew his horn. Burnell laughed harder. Burnell tried to compose himself before Magnus arrived. He failed. When Magnus got there, he knew exactly why Burnell was amused. It was even harder for Burnell to keep it together because Magnus was trying to be cool. Chortling, Burnell said, "Give it up, man, give it up."

With irritation in his voice, Magnus responded, "What? It was your suggestion!"

Burnell, still chuckling, said, "No, I mean the way you're trying to be cool about it. Give that up, seriously; I know how difficult it is to express one's love." Magnus settled down to get a quick bite to eat before he had to go back to work. Burnell sat next to him and put his arm around his shoulder. Then he said, "Good job, man. You took the first step. Let's be patient."

As Magnus worked that day, he attempted to compose a poem in his mind. It wasn't exactly flowing. He swallowed his pride. He asked Burnell and his grandmother for advice. It took about five days for him to finish it. Burnell and Magnus's grandmother were hoping that he would share the finished ballad with them, but he didn't. They weren't going to ask. They didn't want to push it.

On the day Magnus was going to plant the poem, he was nervous while they ate lunch. It was obvious to Burnell. He said, "Go do it now, man. Take a deep breath and go." Magnus fumbled as he took the card out of his lunch box. He stood up, nodded at Burnell, took a deep breath, and started a determined walk to place the ballad under the dream girl's windshield wiper blade. About three minutes later, he was back and sitting next to his friend and co-worker. Burnell was the first to speak, "Find a nice, sweet card, and invite her to meet you at a coffee shop."

Magnus shook his head and said, "This isn't easy." Burnell kept silent. He knew, win or lose, Magnus needed this experience. Magnus didn't waste time. He carefully picked out the right card after work. That night, with help from Dorcus, he wrote in the card. The next morning, after he kissed his grandmother, he asked her to pray for him and the note. Right before lunch, Magnus found Burnell and said, "Here we go." He held up the card. Magnus took a deep breath, and started the now familiar determined walk. Magnus joined Burnell at their spot for lunch. After a few bites, Magnus spoke, "Tomorrow evening, 5:30, at TLC."

"What's TLC?"

While still eating, the love sick guy responded, "Tea, Laughter, and Coffee. It's a small café around 5ᵗʰ and San Jacinto."

Burnell responded, "Catchy." He then offered some advice. "If she shows, just be yourself. You have a lot of really good qualities." This made Magnus feel better.

The young lady didn't know what to do. She didn't feel comfortable confiding in her parents. Her dad was a workaholic and a successful surgeon. Her mother was consumed with the high-society life. Mom couldn't understand her daughter's desire to pour her life into the underprivileged and resist the upper-crust lifestyle. Vera was a very Godly woman. She was the director of the indigent ministry program at the church where this young lady, Andrea, volunteered. Andrea decided to share the note, poem, and dilemma with Vera. Vera was touched, touched that Andrea trusted her like that and touched by the sincerity and words in Magnus's missive and ode. She could tell that he wasn't merely lusting. Vera had keen discernment. Her advice: "Meeting him at the café is safe. There are people around. It's public. I think it'll be okay."

Andrea decided, *What the heck. Nothing ventured, nothing gained. It's just thirty minutes to an hour if it doesn't result in anything.* However, about forty-five minutes before the rendezvous, she received a distressing call from her mother. Her dad had a heart attack. Andrea rushed to the hospital.

Burnell was quiet around Magnus as he moped for a few days. Burnell knew things didn't go well, but he wasn't going to bring up the subject. He waited for the young man to open up when he was ready. After a few days, while eating lunch, Magnus spoke: "Looking at that car hurts."

Burnell responded, "I understand." He patted Magnus on the shoulder only like a true friend can.

"Will this pain go away?" questioned Magnus.

Burnell thoughtfully responded, "It will ease. You probably need to walk away and don't look back. Or… maybe she wanted to, but she couldn't meet you at that time."

This whole situation led to some very interesting conversations between Burnell and Magnus. During lunch, many of their conversations started with the church they faced.

Burnell observed, "Apparently they do a lot of good work on behalf of the poor. I respect that."

Magnus responded, "I don't know. You and I work. Why can't these people work and take care of themselves."

After thoughtful reflection, Burnell said, "We can't judge. We don't know what's gone on in their lives. While you're probably right about most of them, there are a few who have been dealt a series of severe blows from life, and then there are the children. Jesus had a special place in his heart for tykes." This last statement touched Magnus.

A few days later, Magnus thoughtfully said, "I really want to be a good dad someday; kids are cool."

"Fatherhood, good, solid fatherhood, is a very high calling. It's a sacred responsibility from God."

"Woah, dude," said Magnus, "That's a little too responsible!"

"It's true. Most men can have sex and conceive a child, but few men can be a father. There's a huge difference."

At that moment, Burnell and Magnus observed three children walk into the church. Burnell observed, "I feel bad for those kids. They're innocent. They're probably victims of their parents' bad choices." Magnus pondered.

The conversation resumed the next day at lunch. Magnus started, "Children are pretty helpless. Anyone who hurts a child is the worst of the worst, a real piece of s**t ." Burnell agreed. He was also pleased that Magnus was giving this so much thought. He knew he was a special young man with a definite destiny. However, he kept that to himself.

Magnus was at a crossroads in his life. He was a recent graduate from High School. He excelled in academics and football. He could have surmounted even more. However, he had a lapse in judgment and ran with the wrong crowd for a while. Even though, he received a partial football scholarship offer from San Jacinto Junior College. He was torn between three calls: becoming a college student-athlete, taking care of his handicapped grandmother, and the military recruiters from the four branches were pursuing him as well, which he was the most intrigued with. As Dorcus, Francesca, and Magnus sat at the dinner table one night, Dorcus brought up the subject.

She said to Magnus, "My love, I think it's time for you to move on with your life. You have tremendous potential and much life ahead of you." Magnus was undecided and angry. His older brother David moved on when he was eighteen. He's a policeman in Dallas. He has a wife and child. He keeps in touch with the family sporadically but doesn't help support his grandmother. Magnus thinks it's time he does, and he will confront David about it.

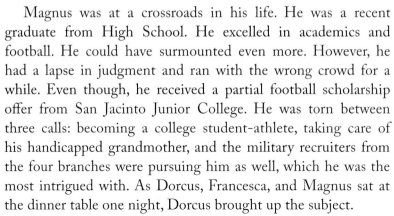

The company that Magnus and Burnell labored for finished their portion of work at the downtown sight across from the well noted church. The new location was ten miles away. The conversation between Dorcus, Burnell, Magnus, and even Magnus's twelve year old sister, Francesca, about Magnus's future continued in fits and starts. One day, while Magnus and Burnell ate lunch at their new spot, Burnell pushed the subject, "What's it going to be, man? Are you going to move on with college, the military?" Magnus was slightly mad, but he knew Burnell was right. He needed to decide.

After thoughtful reflection, Magnus said, "Kids."

Burnell, slightly confused, responded, "Kids?"

"Yeah, kids. They've been on my mind a lot lately, having children of my own, the poor children at the church, and children in general. On one hand, as a military man, in a sense, I would be defending American children, but I'd like to get married and have some of my own. I want to be a good dad. Maybe I'll volunteer at the church."

Burnell snickered and said, "Okay, do we have an ulterior motive? You want another shot with that young lady. I admire your persistence. However, don't play with God and those little children like that."

Magnus came back, "I prefer to call it multi-tasking. Granted, she's still in my heart, but I really feel compassion for those poor children. I know I can't save the world, but maybe I can save a few."

Half joking, half serious, Burnell said, "Maybe you will save the world someday."

CHAPTER 20
THEY MEET... SORT OF

The day came for Magnus to find out about volunteering at St. Paul's Lutheran Church. He was particularly grubby that day. He didn't care. He didn't care if he met her in that state. Magnus was not full of himself. Vera was impressed with Magnus's politeness. That made a very good first impression. However, she would not accept a new volunteer without a thorough interview and background check. He filled out the application, which took ten minutes. Vera came into her office a few minutes later. She apologized, "I had to deal with a small crisis." She constantly dealt with crises. Vera started, "So Magnus, why do you want to volunteer with the poor?"

"We'll, ma'am, my company was working on the new building across the street. A close friend of mine and I ate lunch with a clear view of this church. We observed the people coming in and out of here. My friend, Burnell, is a middle aged man with a lot of wisdom. He helped me realize that being self-centered isn't good. The ultimate purpose in life is to love people around us, to serve them, especially people that can't really do anything for you in return like the people who come here. I think the most helpless are the children. My friend Burnell talked about the law of res... recip... reciprocity. Basically, I think it means, when one gives good, good comes back on them. My grandmother said that the Bible says, 'We reap what we sow.'"

There was a pause. Vera soaked in the answer. Again, she spoke, "These people, especially the children, need consistency. Are you dependable? How long will you be here?"

Very thoughtfully, Magnus responded, "I feel a very strong calling to serve my country, and these children, through the military. However, my dilemma is my legally blind grandmother. I'm helping to take care of her. I believe my sister will fully be of age to help her in a few years. Maybe then I can move on. In the meantime, I'll work and help one or two evenings a week here. I think when you speak with my boss, ma'am, I believe that will verify my dependability."

Vera was convinced. However, she maintained her poker face and let him know she needed to check the application. "I'll contact you in a day or two," concluded the loving director. As she said goodbye, she could hardly contain her excitement at his qualities. The next evening, Vera called Magnus. The first thing she said was, "When can you start?"

Magnus was taken aback, but quickly regained himself. "How about Monday and Thursday. I can be there about 5:30." Once they concluded and Magnus hung up, his heart was still slightly aching. The evening before, when he was at the church, he didn't see her or the Beemer. *Does she no longer volunteer there? Will I ever see her again?* Magnus chuckled to himself as he resigned to it being over for good. *You win some, you lose some.* He would never ask Vera about her. He didn't have to. As he walked up the street toward the church the next time, he saw it—the BMW. A rush of excitement and anxiety hit him all at once. In the church, as he approached Vera's door, it was closed. He patiently waited. A few minutes later, Magnus's dream girl walked out. She had obviously been crying. Vera was right behind her. The girl of Magnus's dreams walked passed him without acknowledging him. Magnus couldn't believe it. He came within two feet of the love of his life. Vera touched Magnus's arm and said to him, "Come on. I'll get you started."

She took him to a small room with two boys and a girl: Blaine—age eight, Alejandro—age eleven, and Gabriella—age nine. Alejandro and Gabriella were siblings. They wore old, obviously cheap clothes, but they were very neat and clean. They were very polite, quiet, and well-behaved. They had a hard working single mother. She was currently at her job. Blaine was more un-groomed and unruly; he came from a very dysfunctional home. His mom's boyfriend was an abusive alcoholic. His family was a mess. He had a brother in prison, a sister who was a prostitute, and another sister who was being sexually abused by the boyfriend. The mother was too weak and scared to do anything about it—an enabler. To Blaine's credit, he went to the church on his own. Magnus helped them with homework. Alejandro and Gabriella needed little assistance and prompting. Blaine, however, was much more high maintenance. Magnus didn't mind though. He was a natural. He was very firm, gentle and patient with Blaine. At the end of the study time, Blaine was fully attached to Magnus.

There was a small playground in the back. All the kids played there until the program ended for the day. Magnus taught Alejandro, Blaine, and Gabriella how to properly throw a football. Blaine threw a wild pass past Magnus. It ended up at the feet of his dream girl. Magnus went to retrieve it, heart pounding. She picked it up and handed it to the grubby, but cute, blue collar worker. Their eyes met, and Magnus coolly said, "Thanks." Andrea smiled. He immediately went back to the game. Both Andrea and Magnus felt a flutter deep down. Andrea couldn't help but notice how well he interacted with the three kids. She was equally gifted at working with the younger children.

At the end of the day, Blaine said to Magnus, "See you tomorrow!"

Magnus responded, "Monday, my man."

"Oh," moaned Blaine, slightly dejected.

The next day at lunch, Magnus shared with Burnell the details of his first day of volunteering. He spent a lot of time describing Blaine. Burnell listened intently then he observed, "I believe that young man needs a stable, strong man in his life. I'm sure he has a messed up home." Burnell was convinced that Magnus's motives for volunteering were right. At first, he was concerned that Magnus had an ulterior intention: the dream girl. In fact, Magnus's heart was in the right place, though she always lingered in there too.

On Saturday, Dorcus, Francesca, and Magnus went shopping. Because of Dorcus' fixed income, and Magnus's minimal wages, the family could not afford a car. They utilized public transportation for their errands. Magnus had a Honda NX 650 motorcycle that he road to work. During their outing, Magnus told Dorcus about the three children. He also told her about Vera. He said, "She reminds me a lot of you, grandma. She's a caring, strong, Godly woman." Dorcus was flattered.

Dorcus asked, "Did you see that young lady?"

Magnus, now acting cool and indifferent responded, "Oh, her? Yeah."

Dorcus smiled and Francesca giggled. Magnus put Francesca in a gentle head lock, and then gave her a noogie. Francesca giggled harder and Dorcus smiled bigger.

Magnus found that Blaine was on his mind more than the dream girl. Dorcus' words were finally sinking in. "Let God pick the right woman for you to marry. Don't try to choose her yourself." Magnus didn't know what was going on in Blaine's life, but he knew it wasn't good. Magnus was looking forward to Monday. He was anxious to mentor Blaine, and if he interacted with her, that would be okay too.

Magnus found a place to park right in front of the now famous Beemer. Magnus went straight to his class room. Alejandro and Gabriella were quietly waiting. Blaine wasn't there. "Hey guys, what kind of homework do you have?" questioned Magnus.

In a polite manner, Alejandro said, "Math," and Gabriella said, "History."

Magnus responded, "Right on! I like both of those subjects."

While Magnus was assisting them both, concern for Blaine was lingering in his mind. He never showed up that day. At the end, Magnus found Vera to ask about Blaine. Vera took him into her office and shut the door. She told him what she knew about the dysfunctional nature of his home life; however, she didn't even know how bad it really was. She told him about the alleged abuse. Vera too, was very concerned about Blaine. There were so many struggling families and individuals who utilized the church's services that she was concerned about. She couldn't correct and save all the sad cases. But she agreed Blaine probably needed intervention.

CHAPTER 21

OPERATION: RESCUE BLAINE

Magnus was excited to see Blaine Thursday. Blaine was more enthusiastic to see Magnus. "Okay, kiddos, let's get to work," ordered Magnus to his three new friends. Blaine had a hard time settling down. Magnus had to redirect him too many times. Finally, because he was disturbing Alejandro and Gabriella, Magnus took him to Vera's office, and explained to her that he was misbehaving. Blaine would spend the rest of the day in her office. A part of Blaine was mad, but another part of him knew he'd crossed the line, pushed the boundary too far. Deep down, he longed for Magnus's attention and discipline. While, Alejandro and Gabriella played outside, Magnus walked over to Andrea and said, "Excuse me, will you please watch those two. They're no trouble. I need to go talk to Blaine."

Andrea, a bit nervous replied, "No problem. I know Blaine can be a handful. I'm glad you're here. He needs a consistent, strong male influence." She was impressed that he was a hardworking, blue collar man.

Magnus coolly said, "Thanks," and walked into the church.

Magnus took Blaine, with Vera's permission, into the sanctuary. The dark, rich wood, deep red cushions, stain glass windows, and cross in front made it a soothing atmosphere. They both sat quietly in the back pew for about a minute. Magnus was collecting his thoughts, and Blaine sat with arms crossed, brow furrowed, and jaw clenched. "Do you know why I took you to Ms. Vera's office?"

Blaine, still maintaining the same angry posture, responded, "Because I bothered Alejandro and Gabriella. I'm a terrible kid."

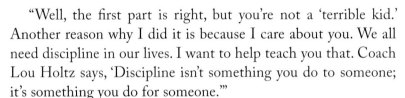

"Well, the first part is right, but you're not a 'terrible kid.' Another reason why I did it is because I care about you. We all need discipline in our lives. I want to help teach you that. Coach Lou Holtz says, 'Discipline isn't something you do to someone; it's something you do for someone.'"

With tears welling up in his eyes, Blaine choked out, "Okay. Sorry I didn't act good today."

Magnus asked, "What are you doing Saturday?"

Blaine uncrossed his arms, straightened up, and said excitedly, "Noth— nothing."

"We'll have lunch and go play catch. I think I can get us into Darrell Royal Stadium, where the Longhorns play. If not, there's a park across the street. Where do you live?"

Blaine was so excited, his eyes brightened. He couldn't say how to get to his house. Magnus took him to find Vera. They found Vera and Andrea standing in the hall. Between the three of them, they gathered what Blaine was saying.

Magnus said to Blaine, "Alright, I'll see you Saturday at 11:00."

Andrea and Magnus walked out of the church at the same time. A conversation began in front. Andrea started, "Please let me know how it goes. I have a similar situation with a little girl a few years younger than Blaine."

Magnus, now feeling about ninety percent at ease talking to Andrea, asked, "How long have you been doing this? Have any insight for me?"

Andrea, also ninety percent at ease talking to Magnus face to face, responded, "About a year and a half. I've been spending one on one time with Sarah for about three months. We've gotten together four or five times. Her mother is a heroin addict. They live ten blocks from here. I don't know; maybe I need insight from you."

Magnus walked her to the car. He was concerned about her. He said, "You better get out of here before it gets dark. See you Monday."

As Andrea said, "Yeah," their eyes locked again.

———————

It was a cloudy, cool day as Magnus drove his motorcycle through the modest to low income neighborhood. As he approached Blaine's house, he clearly saw him sitting on the porch. Blaine jumped up when he recognized Magnus. The small, white wood frame house was badly neglected. There was a chain link fence around it. The so called yard was nothing more than dirt and weeds. It was littered with trash and children's toys. When Blaine saw Magnus approaching, he didn't know what to do. He couldn't contain himself. He started to run to the gate, he stopped, waved, started to run in the house, stopped, ran back to the gate. By this time Magnus was parked and standing there. With wide eyes, Blaine asked, "Do I get to ride on your motorcycle?"

"If it's okay with your parents. If not, we'll have to walk to Congress Avenue and catch the bus. Let's go ask." Magnus assumed that someone in the family would want to meet him and question what his plans were. Sadly, no one cared. When they walked in, a nervous, haggard looking woman made an unsuccessful attempt to straighten up the living room. The place reeked of cigarette smoke, alcohol, dirty diapers, and body odor. It was a pig sty.

Blaine announced proudly, "This is Magnus from the church, remember? We're going to spend the day together, remember?

Without looking at Magnus, she said, "He-he-llo." She made a feeble attempt to straighten her hair and shabby dress.

Just then, a dirty, naked two year old boy came running out of the kitchen, gleefully screaming. He ran into the couch and then he ran into another chair. He was out of control. A man's voice came from a side room with a halfway opened door, "Shut the f**k up!" the mother tried to control the toddler.

Magnus couldn't get out of that chaos quick enough. As he walked out, he said to the woman, "I'll have him home by 4:00." She wasn't paying attention.

Magnus was responsible and heeded his grandmother's wishes. He always wore a motorcycle helmet. He had a slightly smaller one that he carefully strapped on Blaine. The day started out with pizza at Dario's, which was arguably the best in town. Blaine loved it. He had never been there before. Next, Magnus took him to the Capitol Building. Blaine had never been there before either. It was a whole new world for him. It was a day of many, many good firsts for Blaine, and it would ultimately be the day of a new beginning for him as well. They then went to the University of Texas campus. They were able to get into the football stadium. First, they walked and raced around the track. After that, they walked up into the stands and sat. Once they were rested, they climbed to the top. Blaine had never seen Austin from that high vantage point. Blaine was terrified to be so high, but Magnus stayed close and encouraged him. Blaine became more at ease. They sat up there for a long time in silence. Blaine was soaking in the experience. After a while, Magnus said, "Let's go throw the football around."

Blaine couldn't believe he was actually on a real football field. He couldn't get over the fact that the gridiron wasn't actual grass! He kept touching it and exclaiming, "No way! This is so cool!" They started playing a pseudo-football game. Magnus did a good job of tackling Blaine rough enough but not too jarring. At one point, the back of Blaine's shirt rose up, exposing his back; it was riddled with bruises and small scars from cigarette burns.

"How did you get those bruises and scars? Lift up the front of your shirt."

Blaine was nervous, and tears came to his eyes as he started to lift his shirt. About halfway he stopped and put it back down. It was too late; Magnus saw the same bruises and scars. Blaine stammered, "I-I c-can't, he'll really hurt—I mean… he told me not to… if I tell, he'll kill me and my mom… I can't, please." By this time, Blaine was sobbing.

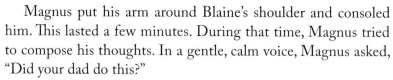

Magnus put his arm around Blaine's shoulder and consoled him. This lasted a few minutes. During that time, Magnus tried to compose his thoughts. In a gentle, calm voice, Magnus asked, "Did your dad do this?"

"No."

"Who did it?"

"My mom's boyfriend; he's been living with us for about two years."

"Does he hurt your mom and brothers and sisters?"

"I think just me because I'm not his own. I think he… he beats my mom too. He yells at her a lot."

Still portraying outer calm, Magnus said, "Let's go get some ice cream at Amy's."

While they were walking to Magnus's motorcycle, Blaine stopped and looked up intently into Magnus's eyes. He said, "Please help me. Please save me."

The time at Amy's was a blur to Magnus. His thoughts were far, far away. He was going to take matters into his own hands and get Blaine out of his abusive situation. When they got to Blaine's residence, as they walked to the front door of his house, Magnus had a determined stride and stare. When they walked in, there was a burly, scruffy, shirtless man sitting in a recliner in front of a TV. He had a beer in his hand and a cigarette in his mouth. As Magnus stared at the man, he told Blaine to go pack his belongings. The man got out of the chair and said, "What the hell!"

"Are you the creep that bruised and scarred Blaine?"

"F**k you, Punk!"

"Answer the question," demanded Magnus with clenched fists.

The man stormed into the kitchen and returned a few seconds later with a large kitchen knife. "Get outta my house!"

Magnus didn't move as he said, "With Blaine." As the man moved toward him, Magnus ripped off the leg of an end table. He didn't hesitate. He caught the child abuser square in the forehead.

The man staggered backwards and stumbled to the floor. The mother looked on with shock. The mother's first instinct was to tend to her boyfriend. She applied paper towels to the wound and tried to caress and comfort him. Magnus said to her, "I'll get you out of this mess too."

Her look went from nervous to almost demonic as she screamed, "F**k you! Get out of here! Take that little f***er with you! We'll sue you!"

Magnus was somewhat shocked and saddened by her response. Magnus yelled toward the back bedroom, "Hurry Blaine!" Magnus was anxious to get out of the chaos. He didn't want to hit the guy again, but he was fully prepared to do so. Suddenly, the mother sprang at Magnus with the kitchen knife. He grabbed her wrist, squeezed and jerked it until she dropped the blade. Then he threw her on the couch. Magnus commanded, "Blaine. Now!" Blaine emerged with a stuffed pillow case.

The mother screamed, "You didn't pay for those clothes or pillow case! They're mine, you Little F***er!" Blaine's eyes were full of tears. When she saw that, she fell to her knees and started wailing, "I didn't mean it baby. I didn't mean it."

Just then, the toddler came out of the back room crying loudly. The creep was moaning emphatically. Magnus was done with this place. He pulled some money out of his pocket, threw it on the floor, and said, "This is for the pillow case, clothes, and a new table—not booze or drugs. Come on Blaine."

————⊷●⊶————

Blaine couldn't believe how calm, orderly, and peaceful the dinner table was at Magnus's home. How could his grandmother and sister be so nice? The house was so clean and organized. People really live like this? Between the warm chocolate milk and hot shower, Blaine felt relaxed and sleepy. He stayed in the shower a long time. *Knock, knock, knock.* "Come on out of there, dude," said Magnus. Blaine was so relaxed he could hardly move. He dragged himself to the comfortable couch that was made up into a neat bed for him. The sheet and pillow case were so clean, and the blanket was so soft and warm. Blaine was asleep within seconds. Blaine had never slept so well. In the morning, the smell of eggs and sausage woke him up. All his clothes and pillow case were clean and folded on the coffee table. Dorcus and Francesca took care of that. Blaine felt like he was in Heaven.

After a nice day of church, lunch, and quality, family time, it didn't take Blaine long to ask the question, "Can I live here?"

Magnus ruffled Blaine's hair and said, "We don't have a lot of money and space, dude. I'll talk to Ms. Vera tomorrow. We'll find you a good place."

The next morning, Magnus briefly explained the situation to his boss, and told him he would be there by lunch. No problem. Magnus was a model employee. Later that morning, sitting in Vera's office, Magnus recounted what happened on Saturday. Vera was torn. A part of her felt Magnus should have reported it to the authorities immediately and let the system take care of it. However, she knew the system was weighed down by bureaucracy. She greatly admired Magnus's take-matters-into-his-own-hands attitude. Ultimately, she knew deep down Magnus did the right thing. She smiled sweetly at both of them. Then she gave Magnus a warm, grandmother embrace. She then moved to Blaine and held him tight and warm. She brought them together for a group hug. She began to pray: "Father, please always keep this precious young boy under the shadow of Your wing, the apple of Your eye. Thank you for Magnus. This is a special young man. Please lead him into the destiny you have for him. Equip him with all he needs to fulfill that calling. Now guide us with Your divine wisdom. How can we best serve Blaine? Help us Lord. Thank you for your Son. It's in His majestic name we pray. Amen."

Vera directed Magnus, "Now, you two go into the kitchen and get yourselves some goodies. Relax. And clean up. No messes," she said this with a wink.

As ordered, Magnus got some snacks, and cleaned up afterwards. He made sure Blaine didn't make a mess. Magnus was respectful. Vera was busy working the phone. It took her thirty minutes to find a good, potential solution. "I've contacted a very good boy's home in Waxahachie, south of Dallas. Mrs. Reeter is the director there. She's quite elderly, but still in excellent health and spirit. She loves what she does. I don't ever see her retiring. She moved from New York several years ago. They will take Blaine. He'll be in excellent hands."

Blaine wasn't convinced. He had tears in his eyes and a confused look on his face. Magnus turned his chair so he could put his hands on Blaine's shoulders. He looked him in the eyes and said, "Hey, look at me. If you can't trust Ms. Vera, who can you trust? I will come visit you. I will also write you, trust me." Blaine nodded and sniffed. "Ms. Vera, can Blaine stay here for the day? I have to get back to work. I told my boss I'd be there by noon."

"Of course."

The next day, Vera and Magnus drove Blaine to Waxahachie, Texas. Vera and Ms. Reeter were of the same mind: Take action first and deal with the paperwork later. True to his word, Magnus would visit Blaine three times before he pursued his military career. After that, he would faithfully write. Blaine would flourish and become a good football player in his own right.

CHAPTER 22

FIRST DATE

During the approximately two hour drive back to Austin from Waxahachie, Vera and Magnus had a good conversation. They got to know one another much better. Magnus felt confident and comfortable with her. He decided to come clean. "I'm not a noble guy."

"Why do you say that?"

Magnus took a deep breath and then started, "I love Alejandro, Gabriella, and Blaine. They've grown on me and there is a part of me that wants to help people, especially kids, but the main reason I started volunteering at the church was Andrea."

Vera contained her glee and smiled. She simply said, "Hm, good choice."

"I'm a poor construction worker, not a rich preppy guy."

Vera responded, "She's a special young lady. She looks deeper than a guy's car, clothes, or wallet." After a pause, Vera asked, "Did you invite her to the café a while back?"

Embarrassed, he admitted, "Yes."

"Well, she was planning on meeting you, but she had to rush to the hospital. Her dad died recently." What emotions! Magnus was on cloud nine. His heart leapt. However, it was tempered with concern and compassion for her loss.

Even though it was much calmer and quiet with only Alejandro and Gabriella at the afterschool program, Magnus missed Blaine. Magnus tactfully explained to them what happened to him and where he was now. He emphasized that things worked out for the best. Blaine was in a much better place. During free time, Andrea and Magnus sat on the same bench while watching their kids. They were both feeling much more comfortable in one another's

presence. Magnus was feeling down about the adventurous weekend. How could people treat their children like that? It was an eye-opening, life changing experience for the future hero.

"Where's Blaine?" questioned Andrea.

"It was quite a weekend. I took him for pizza, we hung out at the Capitol Building, Darrell Royal Stadium, and then we went to Amy's for ice cream." Magnus paused, and then continued, "He had a lot of bruises and scars from cigarette burns. He was being abused by his mother's boyfriend. I got him away from there. He spent the rest of the weekend with my family. Then on Tuesday, Vera and I took him to a very good orphanage in Waxahachie, south of Dallas. Vera set it up, so I know it's trustworthy." Andrea, sensing this was difficult for Magnus, put her hand lightly on his arm. Magnus knew he could share more with her. She would be a good friend. Magnus shook his head and thought out loud, "Why would someone do that to a kid? And the mother! What a piece of work." A couple of youngsters under Andrea's care got into a scuffle. She went to take care of it. Magnus watched her quickly handle the situation with a combination of firmness and gentleness. His love for her—not a superficial puppy love—grew.

The rumors at work were swirling about Magnus. His legend was growing. One of the best stories: he wrestled a gun away from a six foot, four inch, two hundred thirty pound man and then beat him to a pulp to save a family. It was like David and Goliath. Magnus didn't want to tell anyone about his exploits. He didn't want to brag. He was a confident young man, but he possessed humility, a rare trait for a person of his age. He was willing to share more with Burnell. Magnus's friend handed him a homemade cookie from his wife. Burnell asked, "What's the true story, man?"

"The kid I have been telling you about—Blaine, we hung out on Saturday. I happened to see some bruises and almost perfectly round scars on his back—weird. He finally admitted his mom's, or whatever you want to call her, boyfriend was physically abusing him. I wanted to kill the big goon. The goon had the nerve to pull a knife on me when I confronted him. I found a wooden table leg and beat him down. Get this: The mother was pissed at me! I almost clocked her too! I took Blaine to my house. My grandmother and sister took care of him. Then Vera, the awesome director at the church—I think I told you about her—arranged for him to get placed in a boy's home a couple of hours north, northeast of here toward Dallas that has an excellent reputation."

It was obvious to Burnell that Magnus was disillusioned from the boy being abused, disillusioned about humanity. "Evil is a part of this life," started Burnell. "God teaches us that we can't put our hope in this world. This goon put his hope in this place. He expected things to work out his way. When it didn't, he became angry and bitter. He's a miserable man. But that's no excuse." After a couple of bites of lunch, Burnell continued, "Ultimately, everyone is religious. Everyone worships either the Creator or the creation. Everyone has a faith in someone or something. In general, the Atheist's religion is Secular Humanism; and the Agnostic's religion is Hedonism."

Magnus broke in. "Uh, English, please."

"According to Secular Humanism, we are God. We're evolving, getting better. Given enough time, we can solve every problem and create a perfect world. They have faith in evolution and humanity. The Agnostic thinks there is possibly a God, but doesn't give him a second thought. For them, pleasure is all that matters in life, attaining it no matter what it takes. They usually end up very disappointed."

Magnus responded, "The Theory of Evolution doesn't make sense to me. In fact, it violates every scientific principle. The star that supposedly exploded according to the Big Bang Theory; where did it come from? It had to appear out of nothing—poof. Then common sense and science, tells us that only living things produce life. How could a big rock produce an ameba? That's nuts! Some scientists are now saying animals are better parents

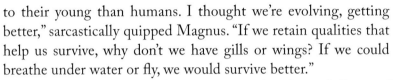

to their young than humans. I thought we're evolving, getting better," sarcastically quipped Magnus. "If we retain qualities that help us survive, why don't we have gills or wings? If we could breathe under water or fly, we would survive better."

Burnell responded, "Then there is the Second Law of Thermodynamics which states, over time everything tends toward decay and weakens. Evolution believes things are getting better, improving. Those who strongly hold on to the belief in evolution are religious zealots. Their religion is Secular Humanism. It's not a big bang, but big BS." Both of them sat silently lost in thought for a couple of minutes. The horn blew; it was time to go back to work.

The afterschool program was uneventful until the end. When it was over, while Magnus was leaving, he met his so called competition outside. Andrea was talking to a young man with a starched, crisp pink oxford shirt, pressed khaki pants, polished dress shoes, and perfectly groomed hair. He was obviously a rich guy. As Andrea and the rich prepster talked next to his Mercedes 300, Magnus was feeling his oats. As he walked by them, he asked her with a confident smirk, "Wouldn't you rather ride on the back of my grungy poor man's motorcycle instead of the inside of this plush Benz? We'll go get a cup a joe." Andrea and "Brad" were both struck by Magnus's boldness. Magnus, not wanting to be disrespectful, introduced himself to Brad and shook his hand. Magnus walked away somewhat pleased with himself. A part of Andrea longed to be with Magnus, on the back of his bike. However, the other part was mad at his cockiness.

After the third day of receiving the cold shoulder from Andrea at the afterschool program, Magnus was starting to think that maybe he had crossed the line. He was so concerned, he decided he better get three trusted opinions: Burnell, his grandmother, and Vera. The consensus: Give her a sincere apology. "What! I didn't do anything wrong!" However, if all three of these confidants agreed, he should probably swallow his pride. Magnus possessed enough humility to listen to them.

At the beginning of the program, Magnus walked up to Andrea with one hand behind his back. He presented a single red rose and handed it to her, then said, "I acted like a jerk. Can we be friends again?" She was touched and softened.

With a smile, she said, "Okay." As Magnus walked to his classroom, they both felt much better.

As Dorcus complimented the way Magnus looked, Francesca giggled. He was wearing his only dress shirt, his only nice pair of pants, and his only pair of dress shoes. Magnus smacked Francesca on the backside with a handy couch pillow. She giggled harder.

Magnus had never been to this very exclusive part of Westlake. He found the gate to Andrea's property. When he pressed the call button, he heard Andrea's unmistakable voice. Magnus said, "Yes, I'm a robber who's come to pillage and plunder."

"You're too late; we've already been pillaged and plundered."

"Oh my, then I'm a superhero who's come to save the day."

As the buzzer sounded, and the gate started to open, Andrea said, "In that case, come on in."

Andrea was standing in front of the beautiful, two story brick home. Magnus easily found a place to park his motorcycle among the high priced cars. As Magnus walked to the porch stairs, both were struck with how good the other looked. Magnus motioned toward his Honda and said, "Easy parking. The advantage of being a poor guy with a bike."

Andrea, ever quick witted, waved her hand across the circular driveway and jokingly came back with, "Plenty of parking space, the advantage of being a rich girl." In fact, she was not comfortable with her wealthy upbringing, but she was at ease enough with Magnus to joke about it.

Inside, during the introductions, Andrea's friends were smitten with how cute Magnus was. Andrea's mother was a bit

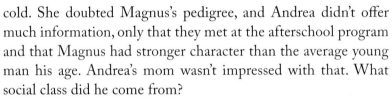

cold. She doubted Magnus's pedigree, and Andrea didn't offer much information, only that they met at the afterschool program and that Magnus had stronger character than the average young man his age. Andrea's mom wasn't impressed with that. What social class did he come from?

Magnus didn't know all the social graces at dinner. No problem. He kept his cool and composure, and simply followed what the others did. After a couple of cocktails, Mrs. Blume, Andrea's mother, couldn't hold her tongue any longer. "So Magnus, what does your father do?"

Magnus, unfazed, responded, "Well, my dad was a spy for the CIA, I think. Seriously, he was always gone. Not much of a father. I was raised by my grandma." Magnus didn't want to dwell on his parents. He went on at length about his grandmother. "She's the strongest woman I've ever met. She's legally blind, but she doesn't let that get her down. She's disappointed she can't work, but that's where I can help. She draws a small disability check. I work to support her, my sister, and myself. My grandmother is a wise, Godly woman. Helping to support her doesn't feel like a burden at all."

While Andrea and her two smitten friends were impressed, Mrs. Blume wasn't. She had to ask, "What neighborhood do you live in?" Andrea shot her mom a dirty look while Magnus graciously answered. She knew her mother's motives. At that moment, Andrea despised high society more than ever. As the tension lingered over dinner, Magnus remained unaffected.

When dinner was over, it was time to relax in the den and let Andrea open her presents. An expensive purse, necklace, and a few healthy gift cards were the norm. And then, Magnus presented his small box. It was beautifully wrapped by Francesca—one of her specialties. Andrea was already touched without opening it yet. It was different from the other gifts she's used to receiving. It was a pink, simple, hand knitted headband-ear warmer. It was made by Dorcus—one of her many specialties. "My grandmother made it for you. I asked her to. She was happy to do it. I thought that during a cold day, watching the kids on the playground might be a bit rough on your ears."

The tears welled in Andrea's eyes. Her friends thought it was sweet. Andrea chocked out a thank you, and quickly composed herself. Mrs. Blume, however, was callous. With a very snotty air, Andrea's mom said to her, with the intention of piercing Magnus, "Well, I'm sure when you and Bradley make up from your little tiff, he will have a wonderfully expensive, extravagant, lovely present for you."

Then, Mrs. Blume asked Magnus, without looking at him, "Magnus, did you know Andrea's boyfriend's father is the president of one of the largest bank chains in Texas? He's very rich and powerful." The cocktails were sure loosening her tongue and way too much for Andrea's liking. Andrea gave her mom an icy stare. The tension in the room was way too thick. No one, including Magnus, could think of an appropriate thing to say to break the mood.

Andrea picked up the phone and dialed. She continued her steely gaze at her mother. This gaze continued through her conversation on the phone. "Hello, Brad. No, it's not a good idea for you to come and visit—in fact, not only tonight, but ever. This last argument was the straw that broke the camel's back. You are not the man I will spend the rest of my life with, therefore, it would be best for us to go in our own different directions. I know you'll do well in life. Take care." She hung up before he had time to respond.

Everyone, especially Mom, was stunned. Magnus was the first to collect his thoughts. He stood, thanked Andrea's mother, said goodnight to her friends and sister, and moved toward the door. Andrea followed him. They sat on the front porch bench. Andrea's hands were trembling. Magnus gently placed his hand on hers. They remained in silence as Andrea's friends trickled out and went home. When they were gone, Andrea spent about an hour talking about her childhood, family, and upbringing. Magnus patiently listened. Then she wanted to hear Magnus's story too, and he obliged. He talked, and she listened intently, for forty-five minutes. Love bloomed. Even though they didn't want this moment to end, it was time for Magnus to leave. As they stood at the door, Magnus moved close, gently took her hand, and said, "Now that Bradley is out of the picture, who is my next competitor?"

She gave him a light kiss on the cheek. As she went inside, she said, "Yourself. I'll see you Monday. Oh, and please tell your grandmother thank you. I love the ear warmer. And please tell Francesca her wrapping was beautiful."

CHAPTER 23

IZANS

In the 1960's, at Folsom State Prison in California, the Aryan Brotherhood was conceived. Initially, they appeared to be nothing more than a gang of white supremacists who were competing with the African American and Latino gangs within the prison walls. However, they grew to other penitentiaries and then grew outside incarcerated confinements. With savvy, smart leadership, they developed an extensive organized crime ring. Their specialties were drugs and prostitution. There was also a code of ethics. Like other career criminals, they often used bullying and intimidation tactics. Occasionally, they "whacked" an opponent to get him out of the way and send a message to competitors. However, initially, a guy's family was off limits. Don't hurt an enemy's loved ones no matter how much he was hated. A rift in the AB developed when this code was broken. Some ruthless ABs thought that it was okay to use whatever means necessary to subdue an enemy, including harming his loved ones. Louis "Snelly" Snellmith was a disciple of this extreme branch.

Snelly grew up in Baytown, Texas, which was a tough, oil refinery town east of Houston. His mother was a prostitute, and he had to raise himself since he was ten. He had seen and learned way too much prior to that age. He never really had a childhood. He was in and out of the juvenile detention center and then the adult correction system. He was not rehabilitated. Being around other inmates served to make him a more knowledgeable criminal and served to widen his connections in the black market network. Snelly had a high IQ and a ruthless streak—a dangerous combination. He had charisma and leadership skills. It didn't take

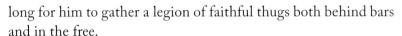

long for him to gather a legion of faithful thugs both behind bars and in the free.

When he was out, he knew how to evade police and feds. He managed to stay one step ahead of the law. He also set his sights on a potentially lucrative market—the rich, white college students at the University of Texas in Austin. With a friend who grew up there, he learned how to exploit Austin in general and the partying, rich college kids specifically. He did it without making them feel fleeced. Yes, Austin proved to be profitable for drug trafficking and prostitution. Now, doing business in Austin required tact. Snelly had to negotiate with the other gangs, primarily the Mexican Mafia and the Texas Syndicate. Snelly showed MM and The Syndicate leaders that, with roughly 60,000 UT college students, there was enough business to go around. Snelly agreed with MM and TS to stay out of East and South Austin, which were strong holds for them.

Francesca's thirteenth birthday party dinner was going to have an extra guest this year. Andrea would be in attendance. Dorcus and Francesca were excited about meeting the young lady that had captured Magnus's heart. When Magnus showed up at Andrea's home on his motorcycle, her mom was beside herself, but she dare not say anything. Her daughter's wings were fully grown and extended. As Magnus handed Andrea a helmet, he said, "You gotta wear this, hold on tight, and don't let your feet dangle."

"Fine," she said as she grabbed it.

It was a wonderful evening. Andrea, Dorcus, and Francesca bonded quickly. Andrea especially loved the baby and childhood pictures of Magnus. The celebration was full of love and laughter. Of course, Francesca had to show Andrea her room. Andrea admired Francesca's doll collection. One in particular that caught her eye was a life size mannequin of a little girl about six years old. It was manufactured by a local doll making company, one of the few that had yet to contract out to cheap, oversees labor.

It was a gift from Magnus. It was one of the first Christmas presents Magnus bought with his own money after landing his current job.

———⊱⊙⊰———

Snelly had the perfect front for his drug smuggling operation. The Hay's Doll Company was a small mom and pop business. It was located in a warehouse complex in Southeast Austin. Burt Hays hated Snelly. Snellmith extorted and strong-armed him into submission. For the sake of his family's safety, employees' safety, and personal safety Burt gave in. Burt was the third generation to own and operate the company that had brought happiness to so many little girls. He was glad his dad and granddad were not alive to have to do business with Louis Snellmith. Snelly was savvy enough to not rely solely on intimidation. He also gave Burt a nice financial incentive. It was a drop in the bucket for Louis' lucrative business. However, Mr. Hays knew it was all part of the control Snelly had over him. He loathed it.

One line assembled life-size, approximately six year-old little girl dolls. The bodies came from Mexico. Roughly one in five had a very small, special marking on the bottom of the left foot. This is the one that Snelly's drug supplier from south of the border stuffed full of marijuana, cocaine, and methamphetamine. This particular doll was plucked off the line and sent to a special location. This was a heavily locked, small room in the back of the plant that only Snelly and a couple of his men could access. The room contained a tunnel with an outlet in an abandoned lot next door, which Hays owned as well. Burt's father built the tunnel for him and his employees during the height of the Cold War in case Russia launched a nuclear attack. The entrance and exit were well concealed. Even if the police raided it, they would only find an empty back room. The doll stuffed with drugs was immediately taken into the tunnel. A guy with a battery powered lamp and the right tools and supplies neatly divided the drugs and carefully wrapped them in pocket size packages.

Richard Johnson, the guy who got the drugs from the doll's body and neatly packaged them, was feeling underappreciated, underpaid, and resentful. He was tired of working in the tunnel. He thought he would be a good leader. Richard overestimated himself. He decided to pocket some of the drugs and sell them on the side. He justified it. *I deserve a little more money, right?* Dumb. Foolish. Stupid. Richard's greed got the best of him. Not only did he overestimate himself, he underestimated Snelly. Like any good business man, Snellmith kept track of his inventory. He realized the numbers weren't adding up; something was amiss. He didn't rant and rave. He quietly set out to discover the discrepancy. He found it, and then he confirmed it. Mr. Snellmith knew how he was going to fix this insubordination and send a clear message to his cronies that this type of behavior wouldn't be tolerated. He was going to have Richard slowly and painfully killed. Johnson would be made an example.

Sarah was a sweet, painfully shy seven-year-old. She was a little small for her age. That might have been due in part to malnutrition. Her mother was a single, drug addict. She never properly took care of her five children, but she had enough love for Sarah, the youngest, to make sure she consistently went to the afterschool program at St. Paul's. Andrea and Sarah had a special bond. Andrea took her under her wing.

Sarah had a few favorite places. One was the Hay's Doll Company. She knew the public transportation system. Whatever little money she could ever get from her mother, she used it to get on the bus, to get away. She often went to Burt Hay's business. The front window displayed the dolls. Sarah would admire them from a distance. She dreamed about dressing, feeding, and hugging a baby mannequin. Sadly, she never had one of her own.

Nearer to Sarah's side of town, there were a few abandoned buildings on the east side of Austin. The non-vacant ones housed bars, liquor stores, and convenient stores. The owners of these establishments were well armed. People that had a death wish might try to rob them. When Sarah didn't have money for the bus, she had a favorite abandoned building close to the projects she lived in. Her "happy place" was a two story, former hotel. It was small but luxurious in its day. There were eighteen rooms downstairs and eighteen rooms upstairs. There was a balcony that went all the way around the inner perimeter. Sarah liked to sit on the second story mezzanine with her feet dangling over the edge. Often, she would sit there and dream about her own doll. She also looked forward with excitement to spending time with Andrea.

On this particular day, she heard a slight commotion and people coming in through the rear door. Sarah crouched and slinked back. She peeked over the edge of the balcony. There were four men. One had his mouth, wrists, and knees bound with duct tape. Sarah was paralyzed with fear. Her heartbeat was pounding rapidly through her whole body. She clearly heard one man doing all the talking. "Rich, Rich, Rich, no one screws Snelly. No one. I'm going to f**k you up bad. Torture, then kill you." With that, Sarah couldn't control a gasp and a flinch, which was heard by those downstairs. All four men looked up in the direction where Sarah was. "There's someone up there. Get 'em!"

Snelly's two accomplices ran up the front stairs. Sarah sprinted down the back stairs and out the door. She frantically ran down the alley. She had a very good head start. The thugs saw her and went in hot pursuit. She was amazingly fast; they barely kept up with her. She dashed under the freeway dividing East Austin from downtown. They finally saw her, after quite a few blocks, dash into St. Paul's Church. The two thugs positioned themselves in order to see all the possible exits. Once the main guy caught his breath, he called Snelly and briefed him on the situation. Not good as far as Snelly was concerned. Who would she tell in the church? This was getting out of hand for Snellmith. In light of this new development, he thought it best not to kill Richard at this time. However, he wanted to put the fear of Snelly into the disloyal associate. Snelly forcefully put the barrel of the gun under Johnson's chin. "I have connections in many places. I will find you. No matter where you go. F****ing with me was the biggest mistake of your life. Leave Austin, in fact, leave Texas, and don't come back." After knocking Richard out with the butt of his pistol, Snelly headed toward the church. His mind was racing. *Who would she tell? Would she be too scared to tell anyone? Did she positively ID anyone?* It was somewhat dark in the hotel, even though it was the afternoon; Snelly felt slight relief from that. Snellmith needed the walk to organize his thoughts.

Snelly had a sweat going by the time he got to the church. It can be quite humid in Austin during April. Austin, Texas, what a city. It's cowboys meets hippies meets preppy university students meets Mexicans meets up and coming musicians. Blues and rock music wafts through Sixth Street at night. With Austin's progressive, young population, Snelly's drug and prostitution business thrived. He was making money hand over fist. He was determined not to let this setback derail him.

When Sarah entered the church, she was crying, scared, shaking, and sweating. She wanted Andrea; she was the only one she could fully communicate with. There was quite a bit of commotion, but Vera managed to get them both calmly and quietly into her office. After much effort and patience, Andrea extracted the full story from Sarah. Andrea, now knowing that men were probably waiting outside, was scared. However, she maintained her calm, which was a source of strength for Sarah. Andrea's first impulse was to call Magnus. Struggling with every word to maintain her composure, Andrea laid out the story for Magnus. "Sarah witnessed a terrible crime. She's here at the church. Very, very scared. I think some bad men are outside waiting for her. Should I call the police? What should I do? Please help."

One of Magnus's greatest strengths was his ability to think clear and quick under pressure. After a five second pause, Magnus said, "I'll be there in twenty minutes." It was quitting time. Magnus had to do some nifty riding and take many short cuts to cut through the rush hour traffic, all the way formulating his plan. First stop, his home; he ran in and quickly reemerged with a duffle bag. After quickly attaching it to his bike, he was off. After arriving at the church, he calmly walked in with the duffle bag. When Vera saw him, she immediately pointed to her office. Vera knew something was seriously wrong with Sarah and Andrea, but she had a program to run. She needed to maintain order. She trusted Andrea, and now Magnus, to take care of it. The day was almost over.

On the opposite street corner, Snelly waited. He too was formulating a plan. Two sharp individuals, Magnus Stone and Louis Snellmith, were planning as the sun went down. Who would make the first move? Snelly called for a vehicle. He wanted it close just in case.

Andrea started to look out the window. Magnus stopped her and said, "Don't do that. If guys are outside watching, we want things to look as normal as possible, business as usual." Andrea and Sarah were confused with the items that Magnus was pulling out of the duffle bag. Then, his command was even more interesting. "Find some other clothes for Sarah. Take her somewhere to change. Bring me the clothes she's now wearing."

In moments, they were back. Sarah was wearing a dress that was a little too big and sneakers. Andrea handed Magnus the requested clothes. Andrea and Sarah were even more confused with what he proceeded to do. Andrea said, "This is so crazy, you must have a good plan."

Magnus shook his head and said, "Let's hope. Maybe you should say a little prayer. Right after I leave, there will probably be a car that follows me. It should have at least two men. You may not be able to tell because the windows might be tinted. If you can, write down the license plate number and get a description of the vehicle. Do all this as discretely as possible. Then, call the

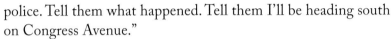

police. Tell them what happened. Tell them I'll be heading south on Congress Avenue."

With a normal gate, Magnus walked out of the church, and mounted his bike. Snelly's thug said, "There he is! And that's the little girl he's carrying piggy back!!"

Snelly ordered, "Be cool. We'll follow them. It doesn't look like he's in a hurry."

Even though it was dusk by now, Andrea was able to get a description of the vehicle and the license plate number. Then she called the police.

"911, what is your emergency? A potential murder suspect? Heading south on Congress Avenue? A white Ford Explorer, license number DVL-666? Following a man and a little girl on a motorcycle? So what's the crime? This really isn't enough. Yes, ma'am, I listened to you, but it doesn't make—I know how to do my job, thank you. I guess I'll have a BOLO put out to the squad cars on Congress Avenue." Click.

In fact, it was enough information. Not only had local authorities been looking for more evidence to get Snelly off the streets, but the FBI has been pursuing him as well. This could be their day.

Between the normal commotion of making sure all the children leave orderly and safely for the day and Sarah's drama, no one paid attention to the man who staggered in and fell face down in front of the church altar. When Vera made a final walk through, she discovered him. She was prepared to give him the routine line: We're not equipped to adequately take care of people under the influence of alcohol or drugs; you should go to the Salvation Army at Eleventh and San Jacinto. If the individual doesn't comply, Vera calls the police. She rarely had to do that. Almost always the drunk or high person complies without incident. If it's really cold outside, Vera will allow them thirty minutes to warm up, and then she'll try to find the poor soul a warm blanket or coat to take with them. As Vera started to give

Richard the standard line, he told her, in between his sobs, he was not under the influence. There was no alcohol on his breath. It didn't take long for her to be convinced he was sober. After a few minutes, he started to gain his composure. Vera patted his shoulder and patiently waited for him to share. He slowly pulled himself up and sat on the same step next to Vera.

"It's time for me to change, ma'am. For real. No games. I've been a criminal most of my life. Today I almost lost my life. Real close—too close. I don't know, I think maybe God is the only way I can change. I can't correct all the wrongs I've done. Maybe I can correct a few. The guy I work for is a bad man. The drugs he sells has destroyed many lives, especially kids. What can I do ma'am? If I snitch, I'll die for sure. I don't know. At this point in my life, maybe it doesn't matter. I'm as low as I can go. What do you think ma'am? I'm asking for help. I don't give a damn—I mean a darn. I'm sorry for cursing ma'am. About this dude I work for, he hates Blacks and Mexicans. In fact, I think he hates his own race. He hates everyone except himself. He only uses people, and he sells his trash to their kids. It's all about the money. He's formed an alliance with the Black and Mexican gang leaders. They all want to make big, illegal money. It's like a marriage of convenience. I hate all this."

Vera was patient. When she felt like it was her turn talk, she gave him wise counsel. Her words were from the heart of a loving grandmother. "You've taken the best, first step: you came to God. He's the only one who can ultimately help us. May I pray for you? What's your name? Richard, okay. Let's pray. Father, Richard is coming to you broken. He wants your help and forgiveness. Richard, do you want Jesus Christ to be the Lord and Savior of your life?" Richard nodded. "Good. Lord, come into his heart. Be the Lord of his life. He desperately wants that. Thank You. Thank You that it is that easy. Like the thief on the cross next to Jesus, all we have to do is acknowledge our sinful nature and ask for Your

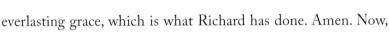

everlasting grace, which is what Richard has done. Amen. Now, we should call the police."

"No ma'am! They'll find out I snitched! They'll kill me for sure!"

"Do you have a family here?" calmly questioned Vera.

"Nah, I've basically burned the bridges with my family."

"Well then, there are witness protection programs. You can move to another faraway place with a new identity, a brand new start in a new place would be the best. You've started a new life tonight, right?"

After thinking long and hard about this, he responded, "Maybe you're right… No, you are right. Let's do it."

Snelly was a big fish. Roger Blake had been after him for a long time. However, Snellmith had managed to stay one step ahead. Blake was the FBI agent assigned to the case. He had a team of four men; that's how big Louis Snellmith had become. The Austin Police Department was frustrated as well. Not only were they unable to nail Snellmith, but they had to cooperate with the feds. However, tonight they were about to receive the break they longed for. Since the foundation of this nation, there has been tension between local, state, and federal authorities. In this case, the APD was competent and good. They were relentless in their pursuit of career criminals. Given enough time, they were confident they could apprehend Snelly. However, in an unintentionally condescending way, the FBI swooped in and thought the APD needed help. According to many of the APD officers and investigators, agent Blake was a good guy. He was able to slightly ease the tension between the FBI and the APD. He was a good leader. Roger had the rare combination of confidence and humility. He appreciated and utilized the APD's expertise and information. All told, though, Snelly was able to keep them at bay. They had to be patient and ready for Snellmith to make a mistake. He finally made a big one, maybe.

Magnus wasn't speeding. Snelly figured the guy didn't realize he was being followed. All of the sudden, as they approached the Congress Street Bridge, a police cruiser came up behind Snelly's vehicle. Snellmith, as if irritated, exhaled rather loudly. Ever ready, he started commanding, "Hand over all your guns and drugs to Bobby. B, when we're on the bridge, throw everything into the lake. Don't miss. Keep one of the guns. Good job, Bobby. Now when we come to the first red light, jump out, and shoot the kid and the guy, through the back and into the heart. I don't know how good those motorcycle helmets are. I don't want to take any chances—through the back, into the heart, got it? Hit 'em a couple of times. Then run like hell. I'll make arrangements to get you out of town, out of the country."

By now, night had engulfed the city. What, happened next was chaos. Bobby executed the plan flawlessly. He quickly got out and rapidly, but coolly, walked up behind the motorcycle and went back and forth from the little girl's back to Magnus's back a couple of times with the GLOK semi-automatic. The bike, along with the two victims, fell to the pavement. Bobby ran between two buildings and was lost in the darkness. The officer in the passenger seat saw the guy get out of the SUV. Then, seconds later, both officers heard four shots. They cautiously approached the SUV, guns drawn.

"Hands up! Get out of the vehicle! Face down! Lie down! Hands behind your head!" Snelly and his two accomplices complied without incident. Once they were secured, and back up police and an ambulance was called, one of the officers checked on the victims.

The officer immediately noticed the driver was moving a little and moaning. After checking him out further, to the officer's amazement, he thought, *What? A bullet proof vest? Why in the world would he be wearing this?* Then he checked what appeared

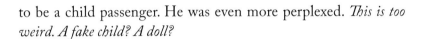

to be a child passenger. He was even more perplexed. *This is too weird. A fake child? A doll?*

Magnus didn't have much of a relationship, or love, for his absent father. Russell J. Stone was an outstanding CIA operative. However, this came at the expense of his family. The only decent memories Magnus had of his dad were in a card board box in the back of his closet. It contained a baseball and baseball glove, a football, three football trophies that Russell earned in his youth, newspaper clippings of his athletic heroics, some pictures of Magnus's dad as a young police officer, his Austin Police Department hat, and an old, worn bullet proof vest. Who knew it would come in handy someday?

Snelly sat in the interrogation room, very relaxed. He knew his lawyer was on the way. The SUV was clean. Bobby got away with the gun. The guy and little girl were dead. The only loose end that needed to be tied up was Richard. Snellmith will have his crooked lawyer take care of that inconvenience. Snelly also had a few friends in the APD. Yeah, Louis Snellmith was confident. However, he didn't know about the two people safely tucked away in another office two floors below him. Roger Blake snuck Sarah and Richard into the building housing the APD headquarters and the FBI Austin branch. Sarah and Richard gave their full accounts. A couple hours later, close to midnight buy now, Agent Blake, six of his agents, a small squad from APD Vice surrounded the Hay's Doll Company, and, of course, Richard Johnson accompanied them. His recollection was perfect. Blake took the lead. He positioned agents and officers at all the exits. Through the tunnel entrance in the abandoned lot, Roger and five police officers stormed the illegal drug facility. It was a major bust. They discovered a quarter of a million dollars, street value, worth of illegal substances. Three men were arrested without resistance.

After the phone call from the alarm security company, Burt Hays struggled out of bed thinking, *One of Snellmith's idiots tripped the alarm.* After he got there, he knew something was amiss. He was escorted to a gray four-door car. He sat in the back seat with Roger Blake. Showing his badge, Agent Blake started, "What's your association with Louis Snellmith?"

Looking totally wiped out, Burt responded after a few moments of rubbing his brow, "If I tell you anything, I'm a dead man." With glassy, red eyes he continued, "They'll harm my family. It's probably too late, they might know I'm talking to you now. I'm in trouble with the FBI now. I'm an accomplice right? I hate the guy. I hate all of this. Can you get my family into a witness protection program if I talk?"

"Yes."

"What about me?"

"With a decent judge? Probably no prison time. Even if you get a jerk judge, maybe, maybe minimal time. I promise I'll do all I can to go to bat for you. I hate this guy too. I've been after him for a long time. We have other key witnesses who already shared very damaging information about Snellmith. One of them helped us bust this drug ring operating out of your business."

"What guarantees can you give me for my family's safety?"

"We'll go to your home now. I'll permanently station two or three agents at your house. When the time comes, they'll escort your family to a new home. They won't leave them until we know they're safe. You'll have thirty to forty five-minutes to pack for a few weeks of seclusion while we go through the court proceedings. I recommend you tell your wife the truth and what the process is. You two decide if you want a warm climate, cool climate, or a mix in a nice, quaint Mid-West town."

Hays responded, "This is too much of a life changing shock to be decided in thirty to forty-five minutes!"

"I know, and I'm sorry, but for the protection of you and your family, time is of the essence."

"Huh. Oh wow—I... okay."

⟶⟶●⟵⟵

Blake walked into the interrogation room, knowing he wouldn't get anything out of Snellmith. Snelly sat there very relaxed. However, Roger Blake was equally confident. He had a few aces up his sleeve that Snelly didn't know about, and Agent Blake was going to keep it that way for a while. "What if I told you we dragged Town Lake, right under the Congress Street Bridge, and we found a few guns. Maybe, we also found some drugs floating close to the bank, and interestingly enough, the cops that were tailing you saw a few things being thrown out of your vehicle."

"Don't insult me. If there were guns in Town Lake, they wouldn't have fingerprints. You have no idea who they belong to." Snelly continued, "My friend might have thrown trash out of the SUV. I'll pay the fine for littering in public, Agent Blake." At that, Snellmith shutdown, no more talk.

As Roger started to walk out, he said, "No, we didn't drag the lake. I don't think we'll need to waste our time." That last statement was like an annoying gnat near Snelly's ear. What did the feds have?

The FBI, in fact, had a slam dunk: Burt Hays's, Sarah's, and Richard's firsthand testimony, Magnus's and Andrea's secondhand testimony, the police officers' eye witness account of what they observed, and a quarter of a million dollars in confiscated drugs. Snelly and six of his men were in custody. Yes, it was the end of the line for Louis Snellmith. For the next several weeks, life was disrupted for the witnesses. They were kept in safehouses in and around Texas. However, it was worth it.

⟶⟶●⟵⟵

Louis Snellmith would die at the age of sixty-three from cancer in a maximum security federal prison in Indiana. His lawyer would constantly struggle, trying to practice honest law. Snelly's thugs, without their leader, couldn't thrive in mainstream society. Bobby would wait like a faithful dog for Snelly to rescue him, to get him far from Austin. He eventually would wander out of the city on his own. He would become a homeless drifter. The authorities would never catch him. However, he would live in a self-induced prison of alcohol and drugs the rest of his life. Snelly and his crew would end their lives ingloriously and sadly. One, though, would become a productive member of society.

Richard Johnson, now William "Bill" Jones, would get a job as a school janitor in a small Kansas town. The change of environment and slower pace would be the best thing for him. He would earn the reputation as a hardworking, quiet, good, church-going man. He would even find a nice gal to settle down with and marry. Sure, there would be a few times that he would almost slip back into his old ways, but his faith and his wife would keep him balanced and steady. Because of those two influences, he would grow stronger from each bout with temptation. He would die a content old man, with three children, six grandchildren, and one great granddaughter.

Sarah's mom, while stuck in the cycle of falling in love with losers, irresponsible money management skills, unhealthy life style, cigarettes, and too much beer, loved her daughter, and wanted the best for Sarah. For better or worse, they weren't going to be separated. With their new identities, they would move to a nice town in Oregon. Unfortunately, it wouldn't take Sarah's mother long to gravitate toward her old ways. One of the local bars would hypnotize her and draw her. Fortunately, Sarah would have enough of Andrea and Vera's influence left in her when she became a teenager. She would submerge herself in her schoolwork and a part-time job. She would have a deep down calling to be a nurse, and she wouldn't be denied. She would arrange to get her own college grants, scholarships, and financial aid. She would do it! She would become a wonderfully competent RN.

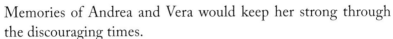

Memories of Andrea and Vera would keep her strong through the discouraging times.

She would marry and have two children. However, her mother's influence would rear its ugly head in her choice of men. Her husband would turn out to be an abusive, cheating, deadbeat. Unlike her mother, though, Sarah would learn from her mistakes. She would be a magnificent, working single mother. After much patience, she would marry again. This time, she would pick a winner.

CHAPTER 24

PUPPY LOVE?

While the eye witnesses, Acacia and Richard, qualified for the witness protection program, the secondary witnesses did not. However, Roger Blake gave Andrea, Dorcus, and Magnus some advice. "If you've considered a major move, a career, or life change now is the time. If you insist on staying in Austin, like Vera, change your daily routine. Moving to another house would be a good idea." Vera didn't change a thing. It's not that she was being bull-headed, she was sixty-eight years old and felt like she had a full, rich life. If it was to be the end, so be it. She was content and ready. It turned out to be erring on the side of caution. Nothing would happen to her. Snelly's operation was so fragmented and defeated that it would eventually dissolve.

Now, what of Magnus and Andrea? Magnus was twenty-two and Andrea was twenty. They were open to exploring the world beyond Central Texas. Sitting on the patio of a quaint, romantic, and small Mexican restaurant in downtown, Austin provided the perfect atmosphere for the topic of the future to naturally arise. They were both finally comfortable and relaxed after the Louis Snellmith trial and conviction. Andrea started, "How did you know you needed a doll about the size of Acacia and a bullet proof vest?"

Magnus was reluctant to talking about his heroics. "I don't know. Instinct, I guess, based on the information you gave me. Plus, I have some knowledge about how criminals work. Burnell tells me a lot about life. In high school, I ran with the wrong crowd until I came to my senses. One of three of my runnin' buddies, my so called 'friends for life,' is in prison. I don't even know about the other two. I don't keep in contact with of them.

I was a crab trying to get out of the boiling pot. They kept trying to pull me down. I finally got out—good riddance to 'em. I would have become a much better football player if I hadn't made bad choices and been more dedicated to school and the game. I regret that. I got the vest from my 'ol man. I have a box in the back of my closet. It contains a few personal items from him—mostly sports stuff. I guess he was a jock. Maybe that's why I screwed up my athletic chances; I don't want to be like him. Crazy that the vest would come in handy. In a strange way, I guess he did help me. He's not a total bum."

"I don't think you should refer to your father as a bum. Regardless of his shortcomings, I think you should forgive him. Who knows what he was dealing with emotionally?"

Magnus, slightly irritated, responded, "Forgive? Forgive? He led my mother to a nervous breakdown! He left his children. Forgive… He worked for the CIA; he was like a spy, I guess. I think he had to abandon his family for our own safety—maybe. But he could have quit the CIA. He had to see the signs that his career was taking its toll on his family. It feels like he chose the CIA over us. Screw that bogus operation! I'll never be a CIA agent.

"Never say never."

The wedding was quaint, romantic, small, and spiritual. It took place at St. Paul's Lutheran Church. Vera was the Maid of Honor, and Burnell was the Best Man. Dorcus was moved to tears; Andrea's mother was insulted. It was a beautiful ceremony.

Magnus, and Andrea's, Army career started in Ft. Campbell, Kentucky and ended at Ft. Benning, Georgia. Staff Sergeant Stone distinguished himself as an excellent Soldier. He would be a Ranger. Andrea embraced her role as an army wife. She volunteered with the Family Readiness Group. She would be a blessing to many struggling wives and children of soldiers. For a few years, things were manageable for Magnus.

My how time flies! "Little" Francesca was now a senior in high school. She aspired to attend college. She earned a partial academic scholarship to a smaller local university. She was going to apply for financial aid, but Magnus didn't want her to go into debt. He would help Francesca with the expenses. Not too long after that, Andrea became pregnant! Granted, it was sweeter rather than bitter, but nevertheless, bittersweet. It would prove to be a major financial stress on the young Stone family. Magnus was in a serious bind. His high operation tempo wouldn't allow him to get a part time job. He had too much pride and compassion for Andrea's pregnancy struggles and FRG responsibilities, which he knew she loved, to ask her to work and bring in some extra income. In time, he saw an opportunity to be a Robin Hood, so to speak. Junior officers were expected to pay for most of their uniforms and gear. He saw a way to help some financially struggling, young commissioned soldiers and make a little extra money for his family. However, there was no justifying it. It involved stealing from the military and the tax payers. Magnus was faced with a serious moral dilemma. Another problem: He would have to trust Specialist York. Intuitively, Magnus knew this would not be a criminal match made in Heaven. However, SPC York was the best, and only, connection to this scheme.

Here's how it worked. Magnus identified a financially struggling junior officer with a family. He found out what gear and uniforms he or she needed. The list was given to SPC York. SPC York, in turn, gave it to his civilian buddy who worked at the Central Issuing Facility there on Ft. Benning. The "order" would be in marked trash bags by the dumpster in the back. Magnus and SPC York picked them up in the dark of night, and they delivered the goods to the young officer. The money was collected, and the dough was divided three ways. It worked well for quite a few months until York started shooting off his mouth too much at local bars and strip joints. This, by far, was the worst period

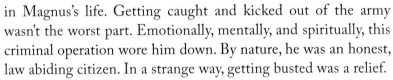
in Magnus's life. Getting caught and kicked out of the army wasn't the worst part. Emotionally, mentally, and spiritually, this criminal operation wore him down. By nature, he was an honest, law abiding citizen. In a strange way, getting busted was a relief.

When he was first incarcerated, that initial visit with Andrea was rock bottom for him. He couldn't control his tears. For the first few minutes, all he could do was squeeze her hand and say, "I'm so sorry." Magnus was truly a broken man. No matter how long it took, Andrea was going to let Magnus speak first. After what seemed like a long time, but was actually two minutes, he spoke. He gathered his thoughts and took a deep breath. "Male ego. Pride, I guess. We were in trouble financially. I know you're not used to that. I wanted to fix it myself. I thought I could, but I failed. I'm a crook now."

"You're not a crook. You're a good, honest, brave, genuine, kind—I could go on and on; the point is, you're a wonderful husband, soon to be father, who made a mistake. You committed a crime trying to take care of us." Putting her hand on her stomach, Andrea said, "I—we forgive you." Please forgive yourself. I am disappointed you didn't talk to me about our financial problems. You can talk to me especially about something like that. I understand, given my upbringing, why you would be hesitant, but please, please, we're a team. I love you very much. We'll get through this."

Get through it they did. She immediately found a job as a receptionist. This was nine to five, Monday through Friday. Then, she got a weekend job as a telemarketer. She went on a tight budget and started getting their finances back on the right path. Things appeared to be looking up. This hope was brief, though. On Andrea's next routine visit to her doctor, things became tense when the nurse couldn't detect the baby's heartbeat. The RN quickly left the room. She came back a few minutes later to perform an ultrasound. No movement was detected. Again, she quickly left. A minute later, the doctor entered. She, too, was

unable to detect a heartbeat and movement. She did more poking, prodding, and testing. She tried to remain calm, but Andrea sensed her concern. Andrea prayed silently, "Please God, no."

The doctor put her hand on Andrea's shoulder and said, "I'm sorry, but you've had a miscarriage." Andrea walked out to the office shaking. It was a surreal moment. How was she going to tell Magnus? He was already as low as he could go. Magnus believed he was being punished by God for committing a crime, and for being a lousy provider for his family. Why do Andrea, Dorcus, Francesca, and their unborn baby have to get sucked into this?

"Take it all out on me!"

Magnus, despite the crime, accumulated an excellent army record and reputation within his chain of command. He was an outstanding soldier who made a bad choice. Those who took time to get to know him, to listen to what his superiors who knew him had to say about him, and to examine his record, forgave him. However, he came across a few too many self-righteous military personnel who wouldn't forgive him for violating the Army Values. Magnus didn't blame them. He was harder on himself than any of them could ever be. Magnus had planned to do at least twenty years in the army for the retirement, but he was chaptered out of the military. Once he finished his punishment under the Unified Military Code of Justice, what was next? His mistake constantly shadowed him? *Is this going to ruin the rest of my life? I deserve it, but my family doesn't. I'll make amends somehow.*

It was not really in their plans, but Andrea and Magnus moved back to Austin. Magnus's old boss with the construction company was happy to hire him again. It was not the same, though. Burnell retired a couple of years ago. No problem. It was a good job. He even got a weekend job at a hardware store. He took care of his wife, Dorcus, and Francesca's part-time education. He even managed to slowly finish his bachelor's degree in criminal justice at Strayer University; he'd started the degree program online a few years ago while still in the army. Andrea was pregnant again!

Andrea was reunited with Vera. She also got a part time job as the administrative assistant at St. Paul's. She continued her volunteer work at the afterschool program and attended church there. Andrea was content. However, Magnus wasn't too happy. Although he tried to hide it, Andrea saw through him. He still had a hard time forgiving himself. He was also apprehensive about the pregnancy. *Will it be another miscarriage? Will the baby be healthy? Do I still need more punishment? Will Andrea be okay?*

On a cool, rainy night, while relaxing at home and watching a movie, Andrea felt it was the right time to bring up the subject. "I sense there is something wrong with you. You don't seem content. You seem a little restless. I don't want to pry, but I love you, and I want you to be happy. If I'm right, is there anything I can do to help?"

"Okay, Dr. Laura."

"No need to be sarcastic."

After a reflexive pause, Magnus said, "My crime haunts me. I thought I'd do twenty years in the Army and then pursue law enforcement, maybe even the FBI. Roger Blake, Agent Blake, was a cool guy. I'd really like to get into law enforcement for the kids ultimately, or I did, anyway. Now my only purpose is to be a working class stiff to support my family, which is okay. That's good I guess."

"You made a mistake. Please forgive yourself; I don't know what the future holds, but I believe God will work it out somehow, someway."

Magnus quickly responded, "Yeah, I think I blew it with The Almighty."

Andrea countered with, "No, remember the story of the prodigal son? Jesus tells this story to help us understand God's love. The youngest son turned away from his father, went his own way. He broke his father's heart. He went to the big city, partied, and blew all his money; he was dirt broke. He decided to go back home and beg his father to take him back as a servant. He didn't expect him to restore him as his son. He blew it, but guess what? As soon as the father recognized him, he embraced his son, and said, 'Welcome home!' It's about 'relationship,' not 'religion.' You didn't have the best example of a dad, but God is, and wants to be, your perfect heavenly Father. You didn't blow it with the Lord, the Army, maybe, but not God."

After a lengthy pause, Magnus said, "By the way, I have some rather interesting news. Remember the notice I got from the post office? It was a certified letter from the Central Intelligence Agency. They want me to meet with them. They sent me a plane ticket, first class, and a hotel reservation for a nice hotel, the Marriot. It's not like a summons or anything; it's more like an invitation."

PART III

ON HIS OWN

CHAPTER 25

NEW HOME

Potomac, Maryland was a quaint, nice town. It didn't take Andrea long to make the best of it. The newest addition to the family, Dawn Esther Stone, was too young to know about moving. As long as she was with Mommy and Daddy, she was fine. Dorcus and Francesca liked their new hometown as well. The Central Intelligent Agency paid well enough that Magnus could afford to move them out there. Andrea wanted Dorcus and Francesca to live with them. She loved them both, and thought it could work. However, Dorcus, in her wisdom, believed Magnus and his immediate family needed their space. She insisted on a nice, small two bedroom apartment close to Magnus's home.

Francesca was able to continue college at George Washington University. That's one of the reasons they chose Potomac; that, and its proximity to Langley, Virginia, which is the headquarters of the CIA. Francesca also blossomed into a beautiful young lady. She definitely turned the boys' heads. Like many "pretty people" it can prove to be a blessing and a curse.

On a splendid early fall day, the leaves were beginning to change, the sky was partially cloudy, the temperature was in the mid-seventies, and the Unconventional Terrorism Division of the CIA was having a picnic in the well-groomed backyard of the director's home. There were roughly forty people in attendance: agents, support personnel, family members, and friends. The food was delicious and the company was equally pleasant. It was a wonderful day for most of the folks.

Rick Munson had been with the agency for nine years. He was one of the agents working with Robert Steele and Magnus on the Muslov Deshnue case. He aspired to be the next Joshua. Though not apparent to others, he was bitter about Magnus receiving the title. *How dare this a** hole waltz in and claim Joshua?* This thought gnawed at him like a persistent cough that never went away and could never be cured. He started with the CIA right out of college. He wasn't impressed with Magnus's Army experience. *I paid my dues. I should be Joshua! They rushed Stone through JOT; he got preferential treatment.* A demon kept resonating this through Rick's mind. Munson was distracted when he saw Magnus's family walk in. *Wow, who's that hot chick with Magnus? It doesn't look like she's with him. It doesn't look like she's his wife. Turn on the charm, she won't be able to resist.*

Munson coolly walked over and gave Magnus and his family a warm greeting. Rick spent a couple of extra seconds on Francesca. He gazed into her eyes and held her hand longer than for a normal introduction. Magnus was a hairpin away from knocking him out. Francesca appeared to be smitten with Rick Munson. A few times during the course of the day, their eyes met. At one point, Magnus walked by Munson and said, more serious than joking, "She's off limits, bro."

"I respect you, Stone, and I'll respect her. She's old enough to make her own decisions, right?"

This time, with a steady gaze, Magnus responded, "She's off limits."

Rick was now equally determined to have her. He would not be denied. The battle was on. Besides the tension between Magnus and Rick, the day was pleasant. The director and his wife were gracious hosts. They created a relaxed, friendly atmosphere. People mingled, got to know each other, and generally enjoyed one another's company. However, not everyone was having a nice time. In fact, ever since the Muslov Deshnue case, Will Vanderburgh had lost his zest for life. Those closest to him noticed how distant he had become. Will, the self-proclaimed nerd, was sitting with his two other techie friends from the department. Rick, acting like the good, self-confident guy who was willing to sit with the

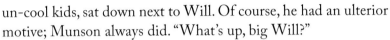

un-cool kids, sat down next to Will. Of course, he had an ulterior motive; Munson always did. "What's up, big Will?"

Will, slightly taken aback that Rick Munson would actually sit down and talk to him, responded, "Not much."

With a very sincere act, Munson drew closer to Will and said, "It has been obvious to many of us that you've been distant lately. I'm here for you, bud. I want you to be okay, happy, content. So what's it like? Traveling through someone's mind? I can only imagine what a rush it would be. With that kind of power, a person could do a lot of good things for humanity."

After some thought, Will responded, "A lot of bad too. It's not as cool as one would think. It's—it's haunting."

Rick put his hand on Will's shoulder and asked, "What's your favorite food?"

"Um, a good steak, I guess."

"Done. What do you have planned for dinner tonight? I want to take you to the best steak house in Bethesda. If tonight isn't good for you, we can pick another good evening. Tonight will work?"

"Yeah, sure."

"Great, we'll leave here in a couple of hours. I'll drive and bring you back here, if that's the most convenient for you." Will nodded in agreement.

Later that evening, the steak was hot and juicy and the beverages cold and refreshing. Will thoroughly enjoyed them. The atmosphere was relaxed and conducive for talking. Everything was just right for Rick to hatch his scheme.

CHAPTER 26

THE TAKEOVER PLAN

"So what's it like to be literally inside someone's mind?"

"Like… like a dream. You know how your dreams are unpredictable and weird? That's what it's like. Or at least that's the closest metaphor I can think of."

"Deshnue wanted to use this power for evil. You and me, Will my man, could do a lot of good. Can you do it? Do you have the ability to infiltrate, or visit someone's mind?"

"Yes. I can do it even better. Nothing against Deshnue; he's a genius, but you know how it goes: lessons learned, work out the bugs. He was a pioneer. In a way, he's my hero, my mentor."

"Hm, how can you improve it?"

"Deshnue's initial model could only connect two people. The equipment and computer program capacity could only accommodate a pair. I've devised a way, I think, to connect more than a duo."

"Interesting. Here's my plan: We get to the director then the Assistant Deputy Director then the Deputy Director, and then, Michael Hayden who meets with the president. What good are these guys doing for humanity? You and I could really benefit the world."

With some emotion in his voice, Will replied, "Muslov wasn't an evil Maniac. He's too smart for this world. If his plan would have succeeded, I think he could have had altruistic motives."

This was working out better than Munson imagined; he'd underestimated Will's naiveté. Could this guy really be so innocent? Rick continued, "We can fulfill that altruism. What kind of materials do you need? Space? Capacity? Let me know. I'll get it for you, big Will."

Will said, "Muslov was easy to track. He didn't account for the large surge of energy that would produce a red flag for someone living in an apartment. This system needs a lot of electricity. People in apartments don't need that much electromagnetism. I need… a warehouse, a place that is accustomed to using massive quantities of voltage."

"A warehouse. Okay, but wouldn't space in an office building work too?"

Um, yeah, I guess you're more of a swank office kind of guy. You know—posh. I'm a geek, warehouse, low key, whatever you want to call it. We merely need a location that wouldn't arouse suspicion."

"Let's do an office building. Our front will be as a computer consulting firm. Our voice message will say we're out of the country working on a project for a foreign company. We'll put a sign on the door that says the same thing. That will account for us never being there during normal business hours. At night and on the weekends, we'll work on 'The Project.'"

Confused, Will responded, "How do we set up a business?"

Rick quickly came back with, "I'll take care of that. I'll apply with the city of Bethesda, the state of Maryland, maybe DC. Lease the right space, set up a phone system, and bingo. We can bring in all the equipment you'll need in broad daylight on the weekends. People will think we're simply moving in. if you have anything that would appear odd, we can box it or crate it— too easy."

"What will we call this… 'business?'"

"How about RW Computer Consulting?"

"Not WR?"

"R comes before W, bud."

"I guess. What about the startup costs? Neither one of us is rich."

"You're a computer gee—I mean wiz. Didn't you see Terminator II? The kid had a special card. He slid it into ATM machines and

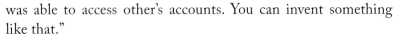

was able to access other's accounts. You can invent something like that."

Will protested, "You mean, steal?"

"Dude. We're like Robin Hood. We'll relieve the rich of their burdensome money for the greater good of humanity."

"I don't know."

"Will… Will, look at me. Look at me. We have a goal. We want to control—body, mind, and soul—The director of the Central Intelligence Agency. Can you imagine what we can accomplish with that kind of power? Our work, our CIA work, is about stopping all these sorry world leaders before they destroy the world. What good we could do in the face of all this corruption! We can be agents of positive change."

Slowly, Will repeated this phrase, "Agents of positive change. I like it. I'm in."

CHAPTER 27

AGENTS OF POSITIVE CHANGE

In an obscure, ten story office building in Washington, DC, Suite 626 had a new occupant. A neatly typed sign squarely placed on the door read:

RW Computer Consulting
"Agents of Positive Change"
(119)611-0666
RWCC@vicast.net

We frequently travel to other countries to assist oversees clients. If no one is here to help you please call or email us and we will respond as soon as possible. Thank you.

The other companies around RWCC rarely gave their new neighbors a second thought. It proved to be an excellent front. Munson started out strong. Behind the unlit lobby, Rick and Will feverishly worked—well, mainly Will. All of the sudden, Will had an alarming thought while setting up the lab. So alarming, he immediately called Rick. "Hey Rick! What about cleaning? Cleaning crews that come into these offices. And Maintenance? What if—"

"Relax. I thought about that. I'm Rick Munson—remember? I explained to the leaser that, due to the sensitive nature of our computer equipment, we have a contract with our own cleaning and maintenance crew for that specific room. I explained that they specialize in taking care of areas with our kind of hardware. They bought it hook, line, and sinker. How's the equipment set up going?"

"Two to three days, one to two if I had some assistance from my partner."

As Rick gazed at the woman in his bed, he said, "Uh, yeah. I'll be there tomorrow night to help. Good night, buddy."

<hr />

Francesca sounded taken aback when she answered the phone and realized it was Rick Munson.

Rick started, "Hello. I'm sure you're busy, so I don't want to take up a lot of your time. Your brother thinks I'm a jerk and with good reason. It's ironic how factors meet. What I mean is: I've been evaluating how I view women, how I'm ready to move on to a more serious phase in life, be more mature. I know I'm starting to get deep on you. This might be a better conversation over a cup of coffee. Do you have a long break between classes tomorrow?"

"Yeah, like between 9:30 and 11:00."

"That coffee shop on campus in the main square, Joe's Jo, is that still there?"

"Oh, yeah."

"I'll see you there after your 9:30 class. I'll be patient. I'm sure you'll be delayed by some smitten young men. Hell! I'm smitten with you. I can't blame them."

"Oh wait, how did you get my number, and how did you know that I'm in college at GWU?"

"It's a CIA thing. See you."

Normally Francesca didn't like foul-mouthed men. She didn't really notice, though. She appeared to have a crush on Mr. Munson. At Joe's Jo the next day, Rick didn't really have a business look, more of a *Men in Black* style, very cool. He wore sleek shades. A number of the college girls wondered who this hot guy was they had never seen before. He sat at a small table, waiting for Francesca.

Francesca recognized him before he recognized her. She nervously said, "Hello."

"It's great to see you. Thanks for agreeing to this. What would you like to drink?"

"Chai tea, please."

"You got it... Here you go. I thought of something we have in common. We both greatly admire and respect your brother. Despite his negative feelings toward me, I hope that someday he and I can break the ice and become friends."

"My big brother has always been protective of me."

"And with good reason. On the inside and out, you're a very beautiful woman. I never believed in love at first sight, but I'm starting to second guess that after seeing you."

"You're quite a smooth-talker."

"Hm, you're on to me, but is it working?"

"Way too early to tell."

"Understood."

"So, I guess you can't tell me exactly what you do at the CIA."

"Not specifically. There are a lot of bad folks in this big 'ol world. I'm supposed to help stop them before they do anything diabolical." At this point, Rick became lost in thought. He continued, "Problem is, sometimes we can't always distinguish between good guy and bad guy."

"Maybe I'm idealistic, but I think we can."

"Oh yeah, how's that?"

"Motives."

Skeptical, Rick responded, "Motives?"

"Yeah, I think it's human nature to want fame, fortune, and power or, in other words, control. Some people want it on a grand scale, some on a smaller one. The question is, though: what are the person's motives for wanting those things?" Francesca paused to let Rick ponder and respond.

"Altruistic purposes, revenge, greed…"

"So if it's altruistic, it's good. My grandmother would call it, love."

"As Tina Turner would say, 'What's love got to do with it?'"

"Yeah, not one of my favorite songs. I think Tina is being a little too—too jaded," Francesca said as she became more comfortable and confident.

"Jaded, interesting word. Besides your beauty and intelligence, there's another quality I find very attractive about you: You're not cynical. I, on the other hand, have seen too much. I'm jaded," stated Rick with another far away look.

Francesca continued, "There's a lot of wisdom in the saying about the glass of water. You know, is it half full or half empty? I choose to look at situations with a glass is half full attitude."

"Me too, but the water is a bit rancid."

"What am I going to do with you?"

"I need saving. I'm sure you're love and affection will do it—kidding. I know, way too fast. But that one was too easy; I had to take it… I'll bid you adieu so you can get back to the books. It would be best if Magnus didn't find out about our rendezvous. I might need some time to convince him that I'm not a complete and total louse, only partially. Talk to you soon." Rick called Francesca again a few days later. The conversation ended with a lunch date being arranged.

Who is Rick Munson? His childhood is very similar to Robert Steele's. Shortly after his birth, Rick bounced around from foster home to foster home until age fifteen. At that time, supposedly, his ex-alcoholic, ex-drug addict mother was capable to raise him, according to child protective services. However, his case worker was more interested in filing Ricky's case than in what was best for the teenage boy. Suzi Munson's drug addicted boyfriend got his testosterone rush by beating Ricky. This lasted almost two years. Burt, the boyfriend, was oblivious to the development of Rick's physique and his wrath. One day, Rick had had it. Burt went too far; he was on life support for about two weeks and barely pulled through. Burt had to eat through a straw for about three months. Ol' Burt would never be the same physically. Rick would never be the same emotionally and mentally.

Munson spent six months in juvenile detention. Since Burt was no longer a threat physically, Suzi wasn't afraid of him. She, along with a neighbor, testified that Rick was defending himself. The prosecution effectively argued that Rick's use of self-defense was excessive. It was. However, Rick turned it on when he was on the witness stand. The tears and the respect he showed to the judge and lawyers made him appear to be a first-class choir boy. He was clean cut and smartly dressed every day of the trial. The jury, and judge, fell in love with the poor, abused young man. He got off with a slap on the wrist. Rick had the gift—the gift of manipulation, couple that with his keen intelligence and charm, and who knows what would happen. To boot, he was athletic and handsome. He was becoming dangerous. How proud he would make so many people: Case workers, coaches, social workers, and teachers! This poor, abused boy, going on to get a college degree and then to work for the Central Intelligence Agency! His moxie! His perseverance! It was, in fact, a feel-good success story.

So what happened? Robert Steele happened. Robert wasn't so impressed with Rick. After all, he too grew up an orphan and achieved great things. Robert wasn't impressed with himself either. A man does what he has to do, regardless of what he has to overcome. Don't expect praise; Robert never did. Rick, however, longed for Robert to pat him on the back. He idolized Steele. This was a classic psychotherapy case study: A boy who was abused by a man, longing for a stable, strong male to give him approval, who had a deep down desire for a father figure. Then, in *waltzes* Magnus Stone. *Magnus Stone!* Not only did he receive the friendship and closeness from Robert that Rick lusted after, Magnus became Robert's protégée! Robert mentored him! *No!* To add insult to injury, Magnus, without paying his dues like Rick did in the CIA, became Joshua. *He goes through Junior Officer Training, goes on one mission, and then, bam, he's Joshua!* Munson was very, very bitter. Rick vowed to have his day. Rick Munson was a classic victim. Nothing was his fault; it was always someone else's. In this case, Magnus Stone was to blame.

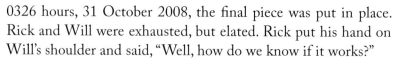

0326 hours, 31 October 2008, the final piece was put in place. Rick and Will were exhausted, but elated. Rick put his hand on Will's shoulder and said, "Well, how do we know if it works?"

"I guess we could test it on a monkey, but we wouldn't get accurate feedback."

"Ah, brain boy has a sense of humor." Will didn't appreciate the "brain boy" comment, but he kept it to himself. He really didn't aspire to be as cool as Rick, but, as cool as Magnus, maybe. Rick said, "I'll bring Francesca here tomorrow after lunch. She'll be well sedated. I'll put her in—which chair?" After Will pointed, Rick finished, "Okay, done."

Reluctantly, Will said, "Then, tomorrow after work, we'll— we'll make the infiltration."

"You sound a little hesitant."

After a long, pensive pause, Will said, "How well have you— we thought out this plan? I mean, why Francesca then Magnus then the director? Why not straight to the director's boss, the DD, and then Mr. Hayden?"

Maybe it was the fatigue. Rick snapped and pinned Will against the wall. "Do not question me again." Will saw the terrifying look in Rick's eyes; he was maniacal. Will was very afraid of Rick at that moment. What did he get himself into? Almost immediately, Rick loosened his grip, straightened Will's shirt, and then said, "Sorry, man. Stress."

Yes, Rick Munson was psychologically compromised, but so was Will. He had his own motives. He wanted to improve on what Muslov Deshnue had done, not so much to upstage him, but to pay him homage. He wanted to honor Deshnue by taking this magnificent idea and making it better. Imitation is the greatest form of flattery, so to speak. Will doubted Rick's plan, but it was a small price to pay in order to create and improve. His conscience was even fine with his money making scheme. They opened the RW Computer Consulting bank account in a smaller, less established local chain of banks. Will correctly surmised they wouldn't have the most sophisticated security software. Will was able to hack into the customer database. Here's the beauty of the plan, which eased Will's conscience about stealing: He only skimmed a few cents from each customer and diverted them into the RW account. The bank had 37,547 accounts. A few pennies times 37,547 each month equaled more than enough to help subsidize the lease and electric bill. In fact, it could prove to be a big money maker. Will was the brains behind the operation. Rick was very smart too, though, hence, the rub. Rick really thought he was the brains. He merely needed Will's expertise with the Mind Infiltration Program, he coined the title himself. Will preferred the word "travel." Either way, Francesca's being was about to be "infiltrated" or "traveled."

CHAPTER 28

WHAT'S WRONG WITH FRANNI?

When Francesca got to the table, there was a chai tea waiting for her. It was a little strange, but nice. She didn't really want a chai before lunch, but she sipped on it. Rick seemed distant, preoccupied. He definitely wasn't his charming self. Francesca was beginning to feel light-headed. She was getting uncomfortable. Rick was cold and aloof, and she was really starting to feel weirder. Rick escorted her out while she could still walk. She vaguely realized she was getting into Rick's car and not her own. She couldn't resist. She mumbled something about, "Wrong car," but she was in no condition to drive. Rick drove to a secluded place and put the now unconscious, precious little sister in a large carrying case with wheels. He went to the RW office and rolled it in without suspicion. He bound her hands and feet to the transport chair, covered her mouth with duct tape, and went back to work.

At the CIA headquarters, Rick gave Will the signal. After work, the two didn't delay. They were at RW consulting in forty minutes. Francesca was starting to arouse, but she was by no means clear headed. Will put the helmet on her. Rick got in his assigned chair and placed the helmet on his head. Will quickly, but coolly, worked on the keyboards. The screens flushed with different colors. Rick grew impatient. "What's taking so long?"

"Nothing. Things are going according to plan. Right on time. Here we go." With the final tap of the Enter button, Francesca and Rick began to convulse. The journey began. It was like an hour long ride on a roller coaster without a cart. The light around

Rick grew brighter while the one surrounding Francesca grew darker. All of the sudden, her ride stopped, and she started to go back. She felt relieved until she realized something or someone was pursuing her. It was a hideous version of Rick Munson that was chasing her! He, or it, easily caught up to her. It was as if he poured through her eye socket. He was inside Francesca. Rick had control, but not as much as he hoped, he would soon discover. For her age, Francesca had amazing inner strength. Nevertheless, she did yield.

Rick drove her back to the restaurant. Francesca, being a physically beautiful young lady with an attractive figure, stirred Rick's lust. He thought he would take advantage of this situation and see how much power he had over her. As he caressed her leg, he said, "Be at my apartment at eight o'clock tonight. Here's the directions."

As she slowly and clumsily got out of his car, she said, "I—I don't know."

Rick jumped out of the car and barked, "You don't know?" This hadn't gone as Rick had anticipated. He quickly got control of himself. He had to remember the big picture, the grander prize. Still, his male ego was bruised. He went for the sweet talk. He gently stroked her hair and said, "You mean so much to me. I want to be with you tonight, please?"

"Okay."

"Okay. See you tonight, mi amour."

She was confused. She really didn't have time to go home and then to Rick's. Such a strange, unknown sensation came over her, lightheaded, dizziness. She desperately wanted to talk to Magnus. *No, he'd over react.* Andrea! Yes, Andrea. Francesca called her beloved sister-in-law.

"Andrea?"

"Franni?"

"Yah, I—I'm feeling really, really strange. I got myself into a… compromising situation with a guy. Well, not yet, but I think it could happen. Can you help me?"

"What do you need me to do?"

"Come with me or take me home or help me get home. I'm not sure."

"Where are you?"

"I'm at the Nuevo Dia café in Bethesda at the intersection of Goldsboro Road and River Road. Please hurry. I'm sorry to bother you like this."

"Don't worry. Magnus loves spending time with Dawn. They'll be alright."

"Magnus can't know. Please."

"I'll try, Franni. I'm not sure."

"Please?"

"Okay. I'll cover it without lying. I'll tell him that I need to help a friend in distress and that she doesn't want me to tell anyone. This is true. I'll see you in twenty to thirty minutes."

"Thanks, Andrea. You're the best."

In the meantime, Francesca was feeling a strong passionate draw toward Rick. *Maybe I should go. No, I can't do that to Andrea. I really want to be with Rick. No! I can't do it. I can't hurt my grandmother and Magnus. I have to be a good influence on my niece, but he's so good looking. No! I won't stiff Andrea.* She was getting weaker. However, she had enough resolve until Andrea arrived. Andrea quickly found her. They embraced.

"Those darn boys," Andrea joked.

"This is a little more serious. Maybe someday I can explain it to you."

"Can you drive?"

"I think so, if you follow me, that would be great."

"Okay. Take it slow and easy. Are you sure you can drive?"

Francesca was much clearer and steadier. She convinced Andrea she would be okay. Off they went with Andrea following. Everything was fine for the first few minutes. However, at an intersection, Francesca took a left when she should have gone straight. Andrea thought, *What's she doing?*

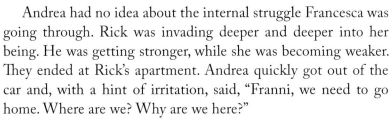

Andrea had no idea about the internal struggle Francesca was going through. Rick was invading deeper and deeper into her being. He was getting stronger, while she was becoming weaker. They ended at Rick's apartment. Andrea quickly got out of the car and, with a hint of irritation, said, "Franni, we need to go home. Where are we? Why are we here?"

"Please come with me or go on home. No. Please don't leave me alone. Don't let me do what I'm about to do."

"What? Franni, you're acting and talking weird. What's gotten into you?"

"Rick. Follow me."

When Rick answered the door he couldn't believe what he saw. He thought, *What the f**k is she doing here? She looks familiar.*

Rick ever cool, though feeling a little muddled, said, "Come in, ladies. You look familiar."

"I think we met at the department picnic. I'm Magnus's wife."

"Of course, please have a seat. I'll be right back."

Rick went into his room and quietly shut the door. He clenched his fist and gritted his teeth. Every muscle in his body was tight. The veins were protruding from his forehead. His face was an angry red. *Think, think! Wait—brilliant! Magnus's sister and wife. I got The director's little pride and joy now right where I want him!*

One of the advantages of working for the CIA was the fun "toys." Who else but a CIA agent would have an ether mister in his apartment? He'll sedate Magnus's wife! Andrea, though very uncomfortable and leery, wasn't ready for Rick to briskly walk up to her and put a mister in her face. Francesca was horrified. In seconds, Andrea was out cold. Rick didn't even have the decency to try and break her fall. Francesca sprang toward her. Andrea fell sideways hard. However, Francesca was able to lessen it a bit. It could have been worse. Francesca demanded, "What are you doing?"

Rick, about to snap, caught himself, smiled, and said, "Who's side are you on?"

With hesitation, Francesca said, "Yours."

Rick quickly got on the phone, "Wilmington. Crank up the machine, baby. I got another. No not yet. Close. I got his wife. Magnus's wife is hot. I'll be there in an hour or two."

In a massive cave, as high as the Empire State Building and as long and as wide as six football fields, demons met. In the middle sat a crude throne made of rock—cold, gray rock. It matched the entire cave. The throne was large enough to seat a nine foot tall demon. Not just any demon, not like the ones who were swirling and attending him, but *the demon*.

His name was Snake. He was one dimensional as well. He was the silhouette of a man wearing a full length, hooded robe. His color was pitch black—beyond pitch black. It was inside a coffin six feet below the ground dark. The servant imps swirling around him looked the same, but smaller—the size of a runty man.

There were eighteen thrones in front of Snake: Six to his left, six to his right, and six facing him. The demons that sat on these thrones were about eight feet tall. There was an air of anticipation. All were waiting for Snake to speak. He sat very still. He was stoic. Finally, he did speak with a low, calm, gravelly voice, "How much longer do I tolerate this imbecile Rick Munson? I'm all for perverted debauchery with Magnus Stone's sister and wife, but this fool, Munson, is going to let his lust ruin our day. He must wait, be patient. Yes, I said it. He must also exercise self-control." This brought muffled gasps from the eighteen elders. Snake continued, "Sound concepts from the enemy's Holy Book. Patience and self-control, we must supplant these… virtues, and use them for our purposes. Since the beginning of time, using the enemy's idiosyncrasies, in a sick, twisted way, has been a most effective ploy for us. Sick and twisted, I love those words. Munson must put his salaciousness on the shelf; we have much bigger fish to fry. Dead fishing Magnus's wife must wait." Snake chuckled at his perceived humor. The eighteen, though they really didn't get it, nervously laughed. Snake pointed toward one of the elders, the silhouette of a shriveled old man. Snake continued to speak, "Asherah here, failed, and now look at him. Good for nothing, really. He allowed Robert Steele to contravene his—our greatest weapon: fear. Mr. Steele had no discomposure for Asherah. How could you let that happen you slimy piece of s**t." Asherah was so decrepit and weak he couldn't look up. He couldn't defend himself. All he could manage was a pathetic wheeze. Snake stood to his feet and resumed. "This 'order' we have, the Elders, I don't like it. Our mas-s-ster, Satan, believes we have become gelatinous, and I agree. We need to go back to savage chaos. Molech, Baal, you two come with me. We will finish this once and for all! We will own and mas-s-ster this computer technology!!"

With a mighty rush and roar, Snake flew away at the speed of light. They even try to highjack light. Molech and Baal followed behind their leader. This indeed is a scary, dark day. In the past, when Snake directly involved himself in a mission Jerusalem fell to Babylon, Christians were savagely murdered in Rome, Africans were exported to the New World, millions of Jews perished at the hand of Hitler, a travesty court decision in Dallas paved the way for the slaughter of unborn babies, and the World Trade Center twin towers were destroyed, killing thousands. Yes, when Snake moved, the operation, from evil's standpoint, was incredibly successful.

Rick had one, big violent twitch. His eyes almost rolled back into his head. He staggered. He regained himself and shook his head. Francesca was bewildered. She also had a sudden feeling of coldness and sadness. Rick said, "We need to get Andrea inconspicuously into my car or yours. You get on one side; I'll get on the other. We'll act like she's passed out drunk."

Rick's car was closest. They got her to the lab without incident. Will was ready. He had a bad feeling about infiltrating

both Francesca and Andrea. He thought, *Magnus is going to be infuriated.*

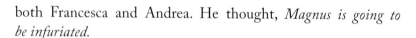

Now, however, Magnus was much more concerned. It was getting late. As Dawn slept, he gently took her to Great Grandma's house. He assumed that Dorcus would be asleep and that Francesca would be awake and studying. He was wrong. When he got there, his grandmother was awake, and Francesca was gone. Dorcus was relieved to see Magnus and Dawn. She said, "I'm really worried about Franni. This isn't like her to be gone so long without letting me know."

"Hm. Andrea is out also. She's been gone too long. Strange. Please take care of Dawn. I'll go find them both. I love you." With a light kiss on his grandmother's cheek, and a lighter one on Dawn's, he was gone. Where to? He had no idea. Where does he start? No idea. *Think, think. Always stay calm, confident, and methodical.*

CHAPTER 29

INTO THE LIGHT

Magnus was formulating his plan in front of his grandmother's apartment when the phone rang. He was hopeful, but it was all for not. It was an electronically altered voice. "I have your wife and your sister. If you want them to remain unharmed, do exactly, exactly what I tell you. You must come to 69100 Virginia Avenue Northwest. No tricks. I know more about surveillance than you ever will. One false move…" Click.

Magnus didn't think he was bluffing. He needed to do this alone. He was going to be well-armed though. The drive was surreal. Who was behind this? *No way Muslov could have escaped Super Max, then traveled all the way from Colorado. It's not Deshnue unless he had an operative on the outside. Highly unlikely. Muslov doesn't operate like that. Is someone trying to get to me out of revenge or my CIA connection? I'm not advanced enough to be a high value target. Maybe it's my proximity to the director. Unless the boob has me mistaken for someone else, it can't be for money.*

As Magnus stood outside the building, the phone rang. The electronic sounding voice called and guided him through the halls. Even though the halls were carpeted and he was wearing sneakers, his footsteps felt heavy and loud. Magnus thought for sure his heartbeat was audible. He was at the door of RW Consulting.

"Enter."

Magnus entered a dark room, 9MM ready. All of the sudden, there was a spraying sound. Magnus immediately held his breath and quickly donned the mini hand-held gas mask, thwarting that attempt. This time, a non-electronically, normal voice came from the darkness, "I knew you'd be ready for that, but I had to give it a shot."

"So, it's revenge, Munson? All this for revenge?"

"Don't flatter yourself. Follow me. I'm going to turn my back. You can jump me, shoot me, or slit my throat. However, if you do any of those, you won't see two people I know mean a great deal to you ever again." Magnus was numb. How he wanted to pounce on Rick, but he knew he needed to be patient and go with the flow. For now.

Patience is good, hesitation is bad. Where did Magnus hear that before? Oh yes, Burnell. Periodically, Burnell spoke of an influential coach in his life, a basketball coach. Burnell credited Coach Castillo with teaching him valuable game and life lessons. When Coach Castillo spoke about offense, he always said, "Take care of the basketball. Make good passes, smart passes, and take good shots. Work the ball around and in until we get the highest percentage shot. Be patient, when you see the opening, the opportunity, don't hesitate. Go for it. Patience is good, hesitation is bad, and that applies not only to basketball but to life. Your breaks, chances, and opportunities will come in life. People have to be patient and wait for them, but when they present themselves, you'd better be ready."

As he followed Rick, that piece of advice floated in his head. When Munson opened the door, what Magnus saw next almost broke him: Andrea and Francesca sitting in surgical chairs and wearing helmets that covered everything except their nose and mouth. Will swiveled around from five computer screens, three keyboards, and a host of other intricate electronic devices. His eyes met Magnus's with an almost apologetic look. There were wires everywhere, some thick, some thin, all in different colors. Magnus quickly knew what was happening. "Alright Munson, what do I need to do to get them back?"

"Let me infiltrate you."

"What guarantee do I have that you will free them?"

Will chimed in, "I'll take care of them, Magnus. I promise."

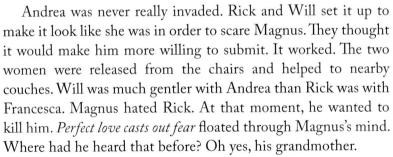

Andrea was never really invaded. Rick and Will set it up to make it look like she was in order to scare Magnus. They thought it would make him more willing to submit. It worked. The two women were released from the chairs and helped to nearby couches. Will was much gentler with Andrea than Rick was with Francesca. Magnus hated Rick. At that moment, he wanted to kill him. *Perfect love casts out fear* floated through Magnus's mind. Where had he heard that before? Oh yes, his grandmother.

Rick barked orders at the women, "Stay there!" They were both woozy and not prone to going anywhere. He then scowled at Magnus, pointed at the chair, and said, "Sit down." Rick loved being in control.

Magnus said, "I want their infiltration reversed first."

"I call the f***ing shots around here, Joshua."

"Yeah, I know, after my wife and sister are safe."

Will spoke up again, "I'll take care of them, Magnus. I'll make sure they're unharmed and freed."

"How can I trust you? What are you doing with this loser?"

Rick pulled out his 9MM and put it to Magnus's head. Rick's lip was quivering with anger. Rick was a man on the edge. After what seemed like a long time, but what was only about ten seconds, Munson backhanded Stone, striking him with the handle of his gun. Magnus took one step back but didn't fall. As he stared at Rick, he spit blood on the floor. Who was really in control? As Magnus walked to the chair, he cleared his mouth and wiped it with his shirt. He sat down and put the helmet on. He knew the drill all too well, unfortunately. Rick placed himself in another seat. Memories rushed back through Magnus's mind: Memories of his last mind trip with Robert. Oh, how he longed for Robert to accompany him on this mission, but Magnus remembered, no matter what he encountered, he couldn't let fear get the best of him. Of course, he didn't know about Snake.

CHAPTER 30

MAGNUS MEETS SNAKE

As Magnus and Rick laid there waiting for Will to type in the calculations and send them on their way, Magnus asked Rick, "So you'll infiltrate me, and you'll make me eliminate a high value target thus triggering a world crisis. Then, you'll step in to save the day, all for a small fee of domination and power and, of course, a few billion dollars?"

Condescendingly, Rick responded, "An over simplification, but if that's how your inferior cognitive skills process it, so be it."

Magnus didn't have to get more clarification. Will pressed the Enter button. Rick and Magnus convulsed. They were off. The nauseating, hour long roller coaster ride without a cart had begun for Rick. For Magnus, it was more like a wait in a cold, gray nothingness. After a while, what seemed like a long time, Magnus saw a speck in the distance. It grew rapidly. It was a human form. Then, all of the sudden, just as soon as Magnus recognized Munson, Rick dove toward him and poured through his left eye. It was complete.

While the transport was happening, Will didn't notice Francesca creeping toward Munson. Vanderburgh was enthralled with the computer screens. She took Rick's gun and snuck into the empty chair. She put the weapon to her head. Was Rick going to make her do the unthinkable and commit suicide? Was it Franni wanting to relieve herself of the misery of having Rick Munson in her being? She yelled Will's name. He was startled at having his name yelled and startled at seeing Francesca in the third chair with a 9MM to her head.

"Transport me into Munson, or I'll splatter my brains all over your lab chair."

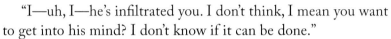

"I—uh, I—he's infiltrated you. I don't think, I mean you want to get into his mind? I don't know if it can be done."

"One, two—if I get to three, you'll have a dead woman in your lab, explain that to the authorities."

"Okay! Okay!" Franni put on the helmet cautiously. She had to keep an eye on Will. He was, in fact, not trying any tricks. He thought he had gone a little mad. He punched in the correct data. He had no idea how it would work though. This was totally out of hand! Will said, "Okay. It's ready."

"If you pull any tricks, and I can't kill myself now, I'll do it sometime, and I'll arrange it to implicate you. I'll cause you serious consequences through my death."

Resigned, Will replied, "No tricks. If this is what you want, I'll do it."

She secured the helmet and sat back. Will hit Enter, and the deed was done. Munson was traveling through Magnus and Francesca's mind, and Franni was traveling through Munson's being directly and Magnus's indirectly. As Will stared at the three of them, lying in the lab chairs, all he could mutter was, "Heaven help us."

—————◆—————

Rick was spit out at a high rise construction sight. He looked back at the round, pulsating light, the entrance and exit, the portal. He then turned to look ahead. Right in the middle of the site was a black statue of Stevie Ray Vaughn, legendary blues musician and Austin, Texas legend. Rick, however, didn't know who it was or where he was. *I don't know where I am, but all I have to do is remember this statue and construction site.*

The ground disappeared. Munson was free falling. He was falling through a beautiful blue sky, with a few billowing clouds that looked like cotton balls. Because of his terror, he didn't notice how pleasant the atmosphere was. Suddenly, the darker than nothingness figure of Snake swooshed by and caught the falling, frightened, up and coming super villain. It was the greatest sense of relief Rick had ever felt. He felt secure, safe. They alighted on the ground. Snake gently set Munson on his feet. Rick was taken aback by the size of the hooded, robed, one dimensional figure, but he was thankful. He owed Snake his life, and the demon would soon make him reconcile his debt, with interest.

Evil looks so inviting. Intoxicating. It takes one's health, money, family, true friends, clothes, house—everything. Then when he or she is lying in the street, bleeding, naked, hungry, thirsty, and cold, the miserable soul reaches up to Satan and says, "I served you totally. I gave you everything. Help me."

Satan will look down on the poor pitiful creature and spit on him or her. He'll laugh and say, "F**k you! This is where I knew you'd end up eventually." The devil then would turn and walk away, leaving the soul shivering in a pile of putrid misery.

Rick Munson had bought into the lie. He thought this awesome figure would give him all he wanted. He bowed before it. "Go to the Gray Cliff," gently commanded Snake.

"How, how do I get there?"

"You'll notice that this beautiful land is flat. This is Magnus S-s-stone." Snake said this with a sigh. The land was actually gray dirt, rock and sky for as far as either side could be seen. He continued, "Land that is procumbent is a little tougher to navigate, not as bad as having to ascend, though. We won't aggrieve about Francesca. You would have to climb up to her Gray Cliff. With Magnus, follow the light, the sun rise, the setting aubade."

The Gray Cliff is the center of the soul, one's control center. It's gray because it's human, inherently bad. For those who have made their peace with God by His son, the journey through one's mind ascends to the Gray Cliff. For those who haven't, the voyage descends. Magnus's plain is level; hence, the reason for Snake's displeasure. The flat trip to the Gray Cliff indicates a person who could go either way in their relationship with the Divine. It's a complex venture. It will take work to get Munson there, but Snake was confident. Not too confident though. He was acute and very smart. He gained his prudence through experience. Mainly the episode of seeing his dead, defeated archenemy walk out of a tomb, totally alive! Neither dead nor defeated, but rather, victorious! Yes, that was an unspeakable blow to the prince of darkness. He learned, however. Thus, he would take every precaution to successfully get Munson to Magnus's Gray Cliff. Time was of the quintessence; there was none to waste.

Rick didn't notice the two accomplices standing at a distance from Snake. Until, however, they approached their leader. Baal whispered some distressing news into Snake's ear. Rick couldn't hear. All he could ascertain was the head demon's reaction, "She did what? Hum, interes-s-sting."

Munson could tell Snake was concerned. He thought, *Who is she? What did she do? Whatever it is, it doesn't sound good.*

In fact, Baal was telling his leader that Francesca had just infiltrated Munson directly. Snake tried to play it off as just a bump in the road. It was more like a hill. Snake grabbed Munson and started a brisk walk. Rick was struggling to keep up. Now, he was being dragged. Rick finally gasped out a question, "May—uh, I—uh, ask—uh, what's wrong?"

Snake slung Rick like a rag doll. Without breaking stride, he held Munson's face six inches away from his own. For a one dimensional, pseudo-being, he had the most horrid, rancid breath. "No you may not." Snake threw Rick like a baseball. As Munson whirled through the air, he heard the last instructions, "Follow the sun!"

Will took a moment to lean back, stretch and ponder out loud; however, this time he sounded a little crazy. "Can you recall your last vivid dream? Did it make sense? Maybe parts of it did. Was it composed of something from your past? Were there colors? Was it foggy? This, again, is what mind travel is like—or is it the soul or, maybe, the spirit? Some philosophers believe the mind and spirit are temporal while the soul is eternal. Some believe

only the mind is temporal. The spirit, maybe, is what sets humans and animals apart. Possibly, the spirit helps us overcome brute instincts. After his journey, Magnus pondered this trichotomy often. He was leaning toward an intermingling of the three, sort of like the ingredients of a confection—distinct yet harmonious. If this is true, the combination of Francesca, Magnus, and Rick is like sugar, flower, and old fish! This journey might even surprise the evil one."

Rick landed rather hard on green grass. It was a park. It took him awhile to pull himself together. Once he did, he saw Magnus throwing a football with a boy. As he got closer, the boy was Rick as a youngster! Rick screamed at the top of his lungs, "Stay away from me, Stone! You Mother F***er!"

When he turned around, he saw a suspended small window. It was floating in midair, head high. When he looked through it, he quickly recognized he was back in the lab, the real world. "Will, what the f**k is happening?!"

Will, after being startled, explained to Munson, "Francesca forced me to transport her into you, or Magnus, or both… This is getting out of control."

"You f***ing a** hole!"

Will snapped this time, he jumped on Munson as he lay in the chair, grabbed him by the collar, and yelled, "F**k you! You f***ed up! You got us into this mess! I tried to tell you not to get so many people involved! Now I call the shots. This is my game!"

During the exchange between Rick and Will, Andrea staggered out of the building. No one noticed. She was starting to get her wits. She sat in the car for a few minutes; she knew she wasn't quite ready to drive. She thought, *Do I call the police? No. I'll go to Dorcus. I'm sure Dawn is there. Thank God. Then Dorcus and I will try to get a hold of the director.*

Munson didn't have a chance to finish the argument. The ground beneath his feet collapsed. This time, he didn't fall. He was being tossed to and fro on a dirt wave. He finally ended up in Muslov Deshnue's combination apartment and lab. Robert was standing there reading some documents; Robert constantly read records. He was meticulous in his preparation for a case. Rick fell at Robert's feet. He wrapped his arms around Robert's ankles. However, Steele didn't respond. Robert didn't even know Rick was there. Munson was clutching a dream. When Rick opened his eyes, he was clutching a bloody corpse. He recoiled in disgust and horror. In all, there were nine fatally wounded people strewn about.

It was a street café in Istanbul, Turkey. It was dusty, hot, and noisy. Rick now remembers sitting there in 1998 with an informant, a sleazy character named Jaul; he had rotten teeth, and he smiled a lot.

An upstart Hezbollah cell thought Munson was going to sell weapons in exchange for cash and high grade opium. In fact, Munson had done a masterful job of convincing the locals that he was a successful arms dealer. He had been in Turkey so long, patiently setting up this sting that his Turkish was getting quite good. Rick's job was to plant a honing device on, or in, one of the vehicles of the terrorist he was to meet. That's it, however, he wanted to do more to impress Robert. Munson planted the device. No one noticed. He hated to see them drive away. They arranged for another meeting place to make the exchange. Munson wasn't going to be a part it. His job was done. He couldn't accept this. He decided to overstep his bounds and pursue them himself.

This mistake led to another, a domino effect. He was sloppy in his distance and concealment. One of the terrorists recognized they were being tailed. They stopped on a busy street. They didn't want the intruder getting any closer to their hideout. They jumped out, guns blazing. The street was full of screaming, scattering people. Rick fired back. He didn't know if he hit terrorists or innocent people. Jaul was close. Rick took advantage of his opportunity and shot and killed the Turkish informant. Jaul could have revealed Rick's blunder, but Munson wouldn't let that happen. He fled the scene on foot and barely escaped. At the scene, there were two wounded terrorists, fifteen wounded innocent bystanders, and nine dead poor souls who were at the wrong place at the wrong time. Robert did the first debriefing with Munson. Steele asked, "How did you end up a mile and a quarter away from the original meeting place?"

"Jaul double-crossed me. He ended up being a double informant. I messed up; I shouldn't have trusted him. Anyway, he said the targets switched the meeting location at the last second in case the original sight was being watched. I didn't trust him, and wouldn't budge. One of the terrorists sat down next to us and confirmed it. At that point, I knew I was in too deep. I couldn't back out so we went to the new location. It was a set-up, an ambush. I hope there weren't innocent casualties."

"There's not a confirmed number yet, but I'm sure there are some."

Robert couldn't find any witnesses to dispute or verify Munson's claim. Throughout the debriefing process, Munson was consistent with his story. Even though he was exonerated, Robert never trusted him from that point forward. He discovered that Jaul was killed by a 9MM, which is what Munson had. Rick said Jaul got caught in the crossfire, but Robert had doubts.

Rick rubbed his eyes. When he opened them, he was in a supermarket, one he didn't recognize. Shortly after standing up, he realized he was naked. The egotistical, vain Munson wasn't disturbed by this. He thought, *These dreams never really bothered me.* However, no one, especially the women, were paying attention to him. This perturbed Munson. He walked up to a woman, tried to get her attention—nothing. No response.

Suddenly, he was sucked out of the door. He lay naked before Snake. He felt embarrassed. Snake questioned, "Are you following the sun? Rhetorical question. No." Snake thrust his fingers toward Rick. A searing pain shot through Rick's body. He had never felt anything like it. It was in his anatomy from his pinky toes to his ear lobes. No part of his body was immune from the excruciating agony. Snake finally quit. Then he reemphasized, "Follow the damn sun! Follow the f***ing phosphorescence! Focus! Concentrate!" Rick gathered his composure and quickly found the source of sunlight. He began walking toward it, staggering. Suddenly, he felt a gentle touch on his shoulder. It was Snake. The demon walked beside him, supported him like a friend. Munson was clothed again.

Snake said, " You know that impish voice that humans have, the one that might express contrary action or thought in one's mind? That's us planting seeds in your mind through our words. Words are powerful. When you speak out to Magnus, auricular, talk to him, you are putting those notions, or inclinations, in his mind. You must keep doing it while you travel to the Gray Cliff. It will get s-s-stronger within him the closer you get. Tell him to get up and call the director. He must meet with him away from the CIA headquarters, sedate him, and consort him to your lab."

With a gentle pat on the shoulder, Snake vanished. Shortly after that, Rick realized the source of light was hard to detect because it was a gloomy, cloudy sky, and he was walking through a maze of crying, Middle Eastern looking children. He was finally starting to gain his composure. Snake's gentleness helped sooth his nerves. Magnus thought, *Okay. I don't know where the sun is, and I have no idea where I am. I'll wait. I'll be patient. Surely this scene will change soon, and the next one will present a clearer, more distinguishable source of sunlight.* Rick was right. No sooner did he blink than the scene changed. He was in a forest, a much different one. The tree trunks were slimy and black, the leaves were dead, and the sky was a dust or smoke filled red like thick, toxic smog. However, there was a distinguishable, red sun. Rick followed it. As he walked, he spoke aloud, "Magnus, get up and call the director. Tell him you need to meet him at the Berkshires Golf Club for nine holes. The tee time is at 11:05. He'll know

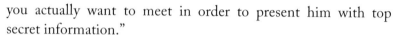
you actually want to meet in order to present him with top secret information."

Rick then saw the floating window. He was anxious to make amends with Will. Once again, Will was startled to hear his name. "Will, man, this place is freaky. What's Magnus doing?"

"He's getting up. He just took off the helmet."

In a slow, groggy manner, Magnus pulled out his phone and dialed the director. He had to lean against the chair. "Yes, Sir, Magnus here. I have a tee time for us at Berkshires at 11:05 for nine holes… Meet you there."

<hr />

Magnus was about an hour early. He parked in the shade and reclined his seat. He was out like a light, not a snooze but a deep sleep. So deep, in fact, he started having a vivid dream. He was at Barton Springs Park in Austin, Texas. It was seventy-two degrees with a rich blue, cloudless sky. It didn't take Magnus long to notice that he was alone. There wasn't a single soul in the park, near or far. No sound of traffic or any kind of commotion. It was eerie, but still, Magnus couldn't get over what a beautiful day it was. Suddenly, three pitch-black objects came swooshing toward him. They stopped right in front of him. He recognized them as being demons. However, the one in the middle was huge! Magnus wasn't afraid of the two at his side, but the one in the middle… He tried not to be scared. Snake spoke in a commanding, yet gentle voice. "Magnus-s-s, I've come to negotiate. The bargaining chip? Your s-s-sister. Yes, she has been infiltrated by Rick Munson. Believe it or not, the rumination of that repulses me almost as much as it does you. Be that as it may, I will free Frances-s-s-ca if you bring me the director. Small price, right? Let's do a quick review, young man. The director was an admirer and friend of your so called father. Your 'ol man." This perturbed Magnus; he can refer to his father as 'ol man, but he didn't like anyone else saying it. Snake continued, "Who drove your mother craz-z-zy and left the family. Then the director sucked you into the same spy life!

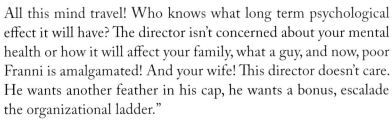
All this mind travel! Who knows what long term psychological effect it will have? The director isn't concerned about your mental health or how it will affect your family, what a guy, and now, poor Franni is amalgamated! And your wife! This director doesn't care. He wants another feather in his cap, he wants a bonus, escalade the organizational ladder."

Magnus knew better, but he did hate the thought of another mind trip especially with Franni and Andrea involved. Of course, Andrea being invaded was a lie–an effective one. Evil is the master of lies.

"How do I go about bringing you the director?" Magnus was by no means committed to doing it. However, he decided to play along for a while.

"This will be much easier than using the nincompoop Munson. Much better and much safer for your sister and wife. Tell the director the factualism. Get him to the lab that way."

"What about the agents that will accompany him?"

Snake wasn't nearly as irritated with Magnus's questions. Besides, he knew intimidation wasn't an effective weapon with Joshua. Instead, he pointed Magnus toward a lifesize hologram nearby. It was Andrea and Franni writhing in pain, gone mad from the long term effects of the infiltration. Even though Magnus knew it was probably a deceptive trick, the image was very disturbing. Now, Magnus was getting flummoxed.

Tap, tap, tap. It was the director knocking on the window. He was concerned at how haggard Joshua looked. "What happened to you?" questioned the director.

Magnus never got his question answered about the agents, but he was going to go with it for now. He responded, "It happened again, Sir. I think Will and Rick—I know Will and Rick have collaborated to recreate and improve Deshnue's mind infiltration technology."

"Do you know where they are?"

"Yes, Sir. They have a lab. They also have my wife and sister. They've been… infiltrated."

The director put his hand on Magnus's shoulder while he contemplated on what to do. Within seconds, the director had his plan. "I only want Pendleton and Bricker to accompany us. This is, for all intents and purposes, a hostage situation. For the safety of Andrea and Francesca, we should go in small, quick, and light. Pendleton and Bricker are the best. The four of us will be an effective team."

"Roger, Sir."

Within thirty minutes, the CIA operatives were sitting at a secluded table in the club house planning the operation: Pendleton and Bricker will be disguised as maintenance workers. They will work on a light fixture in the hallway outside the RW suite. They will be well armed. The toolbox is conducive for this. Bricker and Pendleton will be in place at 1310 hours. The director and Magnus will walk through the front door at 1315 hours. Bricker and Pendleton will bust in right behind them. Bricker will draw his weapon on Munson, and Pendleton will draw his on Vanderburgh.

Right before they closed the plan of action meeting, the director got a phone call "Thank God. Yes. Stay with your grandmother-in-law. Here's Magnus."

"I know they still have Franni. Stay with my grandmother, and Dawn, I love you too." This good news about Andrea strengthened Magnus. It was the boost he needed. Now he could focus on Francesca.

———⟫●⟪———

Snake was giddy, "Only two agents? This is almost too elementary. Okay Rick, this is what you'll speak aloud into Magnus's conscience. Repeat after me, say it loud, 'Conceal your tranquilizer gun. When you approach Bricker and Pendleton's position, nail 'em. Then, pull your 9 mil on the director, force him into the lab, make him get into one of the chairs, then we'll infiltrate him.'"

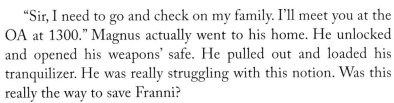

"Sir, I need to go and check on my family. I'll meet you at the OA at 1300." Magnus actually went to his home. He unlocked and opened his weapons' safe. He pulled out and loaded his tranquilizer. He was really struggling with this notion. Was this really the way to save Franni?

Driving to the area of operation, RW Consulting, Magnus was tormented with dilemma: *I can't go through with this. I must, for Franni. No, there's another way. I can't trust the demon. Can I trust Will? Will he free Franni?*

Magnus was sweating when he met the director in the parking lot of the office complex. The director was concerned about him. Could he successfully fulfill the mission? Was Magnus going to be okay? 1313 hours: Time to move. As Magnus and the director approached RW Consulting, Magnus was lost in thought. *The director is probably just trying to fulfill his own ambitions at my— my family's expense. No... Yes... No, he does seem to care about his agents and their families. Screw him. Screw my CIA career. This is for Franni.*

Bricker and Pendleton were in view. Snake exhorted Munson; Munson screamed into Magnus. Magnus put his hand on the handle of the tranquilizer. Bricker and Pendleton were within range. There were no bystanders in the hallway.

Now! Now! Now!

No. I can't.

The director and Magnus walked by the two agents. The director's plan would be carried-out. The plan of action worked well. Vanderburgh and Munson were quickly subdued. Magnus was more than eager to play the bad cop, especially as he caught glimpses of Franni in the lab chair.

Snake shook his head and said, "Well, well, well, he couldn't go through it. He may be more indigestible than we thought. Pity, Mr. Stone will regret this especially after we get through tormenting his s-s-sweet little sister. We will annihilate her from the inside, and Stone will witness the slow, torturous death. Come on Baal and Molech. Let's infect Frances-s-sca."

CHAPTER 31

SINK OR SWIM

Francesca alighted in her beloved grandmother's house. She was in the clean, humble, orderly living room; there were so many wonderful memories in this place. Franni felt good as she walked through her Austin, Texas, childhood home. She went into her room to behold her doll collection. Each one was carefully placed in the bookcase. The walls in the entire house were fresh and white. Magnus ensured the paint jobs on the inside and outside were always timely. Francesca's room was decorated with bright colors. The bed spread, pillows, and pictures were an array of blues, greens, pinks, reds, and yellows. Franni sat on the bed to bask in her happy-place. Suddenly, a hideous hand came out from under the bed and grabbed her ankle. Franni screamed and struggled. Unlike nightmares, she couldn't wake up or get away. She was dragged under the bed. In a cold darkness, grotesque hands kept pawing her. Then they started clawing her flesh with their disfigured nails. There was only one thing she could think to do. "God, Lord Jesus, help me!"

At this, she heard blood curdling screams. But thankfully, the hands vanished. She was lying on a beautiful beach. The warmth of the sun was refreshing. The sound of the waves soothed her. She didn't want to move. It was so relaxing. She closed her eyes and enjoyed the warm water caressing her flesh in gentle waves. When she opened them, she recoiled. It wasn't blue, green ocean water anymore, but rather, filthy, polluted water. She turned and ran away from the beach as fast as she could. Immediately, it was no longer a beautiful coast. The scene was a gloomy forest. There was also a terrible stench. The worst was yet to come. Before she knew it, she was right in front of a tree with a corpse hanging from a noose. It was her grandmother! Franni collapsed in horror. She struggled to her hands and knees. She was about to break: *No. This must be an illusion from Satan. He's trying to paralyze me with fear. Grandma taught me not to fear him. The power of light is much more powerful than the power of darkness.*

Francesca had remembered a valuable lesson from her grandmother. Dorcus had taught her, "There really is no such thing as darkness, only the absence of light. We had to invent, I guess, a word for the absence of light. So man called it darkness. When we turn on a light switch in a dark room, what happens? The darkness must flee. When the sun goes down, the darkness can come out, but when the sun rises, the darkness must desist. Light has total dominance over darkness. God reigns over evil. For His grand purpose, the Lord allows evil, Satan, to have his time. However, it won't last."

Franni forced out the words, "No. Evil couldn't do this to my grandmother. Greater is He that is in her, than he that is in the world. Greater is He that is in me, than he that is in the world." With a renewed strength, she stood to her feet. In fact, the image was gone. However, she was still in the gray, clammy forest.

Hovering above, like a chess master studying the board, Snake was contemplating his next move, albeit, he was a bit concerned. He'd under estimated Francesca's faith, her inner strength. He thought out loud to Baal and Molech. "Hm, okay. Dorcus-s-s has lived a long, unexpurgated life. We completely lost her a long time ago. She fulfilled her—I hate to say it, but she fulfilled her purpose for our damn enemy. Maybe, deep down Francesca knows this, and can let her go. Ah, but little Dawn, surely this will eradicate her."

Up ahead, still in the dark forest, Franni heard a little baby scream. She ran toward it. Suddenly she came to a clearing. Little Dawn was sitting, crying, and screaming. She was terrified. Ferocious, hideous dogs, with flame-red eyes and dripping teeth had her surrounded. They were moving in for the kill. As

Francesca tried to run and grab her, she froze. She couldn't move. Suddenly, the dogs pounced. "Oh God, why am I here? This is only a dream, a nightmare, right? This isn't real, right? Help me, Lord. Jesus. Jesus. Jesus."

Thankfully, the image was gone. However, Francesca was so exhausted she could barely move. She fell to the ground. She felt numb. She was anticipating the next horrible image. Next, she was in the back seat of a car. Dawn was strapped in a car seat next to her, Andrea was in the passenger seat, and Magnus was driving. They were traveling along a beautiful mountain road. The weather and conversation were delightful. Francesca was about to let her guard down and relax when—*pow!* One of the tires blew out. The pleasantness turned to horrid screams as the car careened off the side of the mountain. All of the sudden, everything started moving in slow motion. As the car flipped, Francesca stayed completely awake and conscience. She witnessed everything in delayed time. The other three were being flipped like rag dolls. Objects in the car suddenly became deadly projectiles. Francesca witnessed all the blows to her beloved family. And the noise! Crash! Bang! Thud! Finally the car, or what was left of it, came to rest.

Back in the real world, Francesca was causing great concern. She was screaming and sweating profusely. She held her hands in front of her. They were rigid, shaking, and stiff. She kept screaming, "No! No! No!"

Magnus grabbed Will and growled, "Bring her back."

"I'll do everything I can to get a portal in close proximity to her. If she checks in with us, I can direct her toward it. I don't know. I'll try. I promise. I'll try."

Magnus shoved him toward the computer and ordered, "Get to work."

Magnus decided to constantly speak to Francesca and wipe her forehead, "Hang in there, Franni. Listen, little sis, when you see a suspended window, I mean suspended in thin air, look through it. I'll be on the other side. We'll try to direct you to the portal.

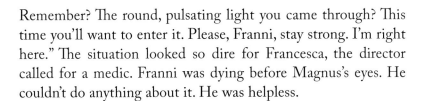

Remember? The round, pulsating light you came through? This time you'll want to enter it. Please, Franni, stay strong. I'm right here." The situation looked so dire for Francesca, the director called for a medic. Franni was dying before Magnus's eyes. He couldn't do anything about it. He was helpless.

After a prayer for strength, Francesca forced herself not to look at her dead loved ones. She thought, *This is only a dream.* She struggled out of the car and proceeded to stagger away from it as far and as fast as she could.

In a reflexive action, Snake punched Baal into another galaxy. He happened to be standing in the wrong place at the wrong time. Snake's anger boiled over into uncontrolled rage, "Where is this b***h getting her inner strength from?"

Snake's pre-occupation with destroying Francesca caused him to lose sight of Rick. Munson had lost visibility of the light and had wandered into his ultimate fantasy: seventy virgins and all the wine he could drink for eternity. He admired the Islamic extremists for this concept. He would never, never leave there; he was trapped forever.

Rick Munson would end up in a mental institution. At first, the look on his face would be pleasant. However, as the years would wear on, his demeanor would become more and more pained and tortured looking. Apparently, the world of perpetual, hedonistic pleasure became, in fact, cruel torture…hell. Many years later, Munson would die in a raging, screaming fit.

Even though Francesca was stumbling through a dark forest, she saw a dim light ahead. Always go toward the light. The light was shining on—Annie! Annie was her favorite doll that Magnus used many years ago! Annie was pointing to the right. Franni said, "Thank you, my old friend."

Now, Francesca was walking down Congress Avenue toward the Texas State Capitol Building. She, Dorcus, and Magnus used to love walking down that avenue, past the eclectic restaurants and shops. It was dawn; the sun was starting to rise. Francesca came upon a window, head high, suspended in midair. She thought, *How strange.*

She looked through it. She said with a combination of excitement and fatigue, "Magnus!"

Magnus quickly bottled his volcanic emotions. He said to her, "You know when you get back here, I'm going to kick your butt, right?"

"Yeah, yeah—all talk. Speaking of, how do I get out of here?"

"Remember the upright, circular, pulsating light, eight feet by eight feet? That's the entry and exit portal. You have to get back to that. You should have some memories that will point you in the right direction."

Francesca thought out loud, "Like Annie. Hm—the portal. Where have I heard that before? It's like déjà vu. Okay, I'm off to find the portal. I love you."

In the lab, everything seemed to be fine for twenty minutes, but that would drastically change. Again, not only was Francesca rigid, stiff, and sweating, but this time, she was convulsing. What was she experiencing? Magnus quickly got into one of the other lab chairs, secured the helmet, and after a deep breath, he ordered Will, "Send me into my sister."

CHAPTER 32

SNAKE'S LAST MASSIVE SALVO

When Francesca turned away from the window, she was face to face with Snake. After both beings studied one another for a few seconds, Snake spoke, "It's over. No portal. No reminiscence to point you in the right direction. There is no right direction, only hell from now on—behold!" This last sentence roared like intense thunder. Snake waved his hand, and huge hologram images surrounded Francesca as she fell to the ground at the force of the evil one's voice. One was the previous image of her lynched grandmother, while the second was the former scene after the traffic accident involving Magnus, Andrea, and Dawn. She had already dealt with these, so they weren't quite as shocking.

However, the third one would be particularly disturbing to Francesca. The scene was the inside of a small church. Between the rich wooden pews, altar, the crimson carpet, pew cushions, and the wooden cross hanging up front, the atmosphere was warm and inviting, and there was an extra touch. Lining the front were beautiful flowers of all colors and kinds in cream colored vases. They were perfectly arranged. Francesca's vantage point was from the back left. The church was about half full. A distinguished looking young man in a black tux and a minister positioned themselves in the front. Shortly after that, Franni's favorite classic song began to play: "Always and Forever" originally by Heatwave, though Franni loved the rendition by Luther Vandross:

> Always and forever
> Each moment with you
> Is just like a dream to me

That somehow came true
And I know tomorrow
Will still be the same
'Cause we get a life of love
that won't ever change and
Everyday love me your own special way
Melt my heart away with a smile
Take time to tell me you really care/And we'll share
    tomorrow together
Ooh baby, I'll always love you forever
Ever, ever, ever

As the song faded, a woman in a gorgeous wedding dress proceeded to walk the aisle. Then, the "Wedding March" began. Her face was veiled. Strange, no one stood or even looked toward her, they continued to stare forward, and the bride had no one to accompany her. It was rather sad. Francesca thought so. It got worse. The minister began. "Dearly beloved, we are here to join in holy matrimony this saintly, patient, and generous man with this tramp that no one else will have." The guests snickered.

Francesca thought, *What a terrible thing to say!* The wedding proceeded relatively normally. The bride repeated traditional vows. However, the groom had written his own. Francesca mused, *How romantic.*

Francesca was shocked at what came out of his mouth. "You are simply an object of my pleasure. I will enjoy you that way until I grow tired of you, then I'll discard you like the piece of trash you are. During that time, you will cook me gourmet meals and keep the house spotless. You will do this after your full-time job."

Francesca dropped to her knees in disbelief. She thought, *Why is she subjecting herself to this? Is this a sick, sick joke?*

Then, the most appalling part of this whole scene, after the minister told the groom he could kiss the bride, he lifted the vale, and it was Francesca! Her heart jumped to her throat. The groom gave the bride anything but a sweet kiss. The guests cheered and laughed. The laughter screeched in Franni's ears. She covered them, but it was no use. Suddenly, it stopped. Snake stood behind Francesca with his hands behind his back. He bent down toward her and said, "You see my dear, you have no hope. How tragic to have no hope. Hope is what sustains you humans. Without it—hell." This last word came out of his throat like sandpaper. He continued, "Lest you're ruminating about what your sweet, misguided grandmother taught you, things like: 'Don't fear Satan. The Almighty has the ultimate power. You're a daughter of the Living God, therefore, the devil can't touch you'—blah, blah, blah. Don't forget, your Almighty has given Satan authority on earth. And we believe, we know that someday we can s-s-subdue heaven and earth. Given enough time, just like evolution, anything is possible. So, I can and will control what you see. You will have a miserable existence here. Allow me to show you more."

The next scene was the romantic Riverwalk in San Antonio, Texas. Francesca loves it. San Antonio is one of her favorite places on earth. It was a perfectly cool spring day in the late afternoon. Francesca and her new husband were walking hand in hand down the old stone walkway along the lazy, green river. The light sound of mariachi music played in the distance. Other lovebirds walked slowly along the path, not a care in the world. Francesca thought, *Maybe he's changed. He's realized how cruel he's been.* Just as this hope cautiously started to peak out, the louse shoved her into the river, right in front of a tourist boat. She barely escaped being struck by the propeller.

Once again, annoying laughter came from the witnesses. Instead of helping her out, the so called husband called her a few choice words and walked away. The actual Francesca was incensed. She said, "No, Mr. demon, I won't marry this jerk. In the name of Jesus I won't!"

Snake and Molech had to cover their ears. Once the searing pain stopped, Snake pulled himself together. Molech was a little more shaken.

Snake assured him, "I halfway expected this. The b***h does have some resiliency. However, what she'll see next will crush her for good. It involves her future children. The maternal instinct and nature within her won't be able to withstand this next, and final, scene."

Magnus exited the portal into a cold, dark and lifeless valley. In this valley were thousands, maybe millions of demons, demons as far as the eye could see. Magnus climbed upon a rock to get a different perspective. It was even more daunting. Again, black hole-grade black, one dimensional, hooded beings as far as the eye could see to the left and right. However, on top of the mountain range on the other side of the valley, Magnus saw a bright light like a star. He knew that's where he needed to go. Small problem: He had to go through the sea of imps. He had experience with this fear, and it was Franni he had to save. He took a deep breath, tilted his head down slightly, and began to jog right through the archfiends. He looked up periodically to make sure he was headed toward the luminosity. The demons, dismayed and shocked at Magnus's boldness, parted for him like the Red Sea. There was a hushed clamor, "He doesn't fear us."

As Magnus approached the light, he felt strong. He climbed and climbed for twenty minutes. When he recognized the source, his hope and strength blossomed, despite the long difficult assent. It was Robert! He looked angelic and majestic in a white robe. Robert didn't say anything. He merely pointed to the right, signaling to Magnus which way to go. The image of Robert only lasted a few seconds, and then he vanished. Magnus headed out with a new determination. Suddenly he, too, found himself on the San Antoinio Riverwalk! Wow! First, the wonderful image of Robert, and now, one of his favorite places in the world also!

Years ago, Dorcus, Franni, and he had come here a half dozen times. They would usually eat Mexican food at their favorite restaurant. Sometimes they would eat German cookery. Years

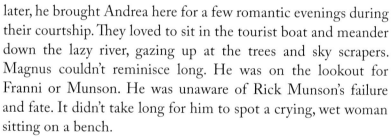
later, he brought Andrea here for a few romantic evenings during their courtship. They loved to sit in the tourist boat and meander down the lazy river, gazing up at the trees and sky scrapers. Magnus couldn't reminisce long. He was on the lookout for Franni or Munson. He was unaware of Rick Munson's failure and fate. It didn't take long for him to spot a crying, wet woman sitting on a bench.

As he approached, he recognized his sister, "Franni!" She didn't hear him. When he got five yards away. Thump! He hit an invisible wall. He heard a hideous chuckle. As if over a crystal clear loud speaker, he heard the voice of Snake, "How splendid! So kind of you to join us Magnus or should I call you, 'Joshua?' You've come to witness, from the inside, the total destruction of your s-s-i-s-ster. I couldn't have orchestrated this any better. Oh well, yes, I could have. I'm being much too modest." Snake was pleased with himself and the situation.

The scene changed. Francesca and Magnus were watching it all unfold, but Francesca was unaware of Magnus's presence. In defiance, Francesca whispered, "I won't marry that man."

"Hm, very well. I guess you can control that. However, your kid-s-s-s. You can't be with them, protect them, unceasingly. Check out this last, final glimpse of your future."

This next holographic image was an intensive care unit. A child of about four or five lay in bed, pale and bald. Francesca can't tell if it's a boy or girl. The poor thing is heaving for air, writhing in pain, beyond crying. Francesca sees herself kneeling by the bed, praying and clutching the delicate little hand. Once again, with his hands folded behind him, Snake leaned over to speak softly to Francesca, "The poor thing is—will suffer from canc-c-c-er. She will not be cured. Your daughter will be in excruciating pain and die a slow death. Oh yes, I will array it."

Francesca began to shake as the scene changed again. This time, it was three young teenage boys sitting in a car. The one in the driver's seat didn't look old enough to drive. He favored

Magnus, so she rightly assumed this was her future son. They were passing around, sharing a joint and liquor bottle. One of the boys in the back seat was the first to speak, "Dude, I'm sorry to hear about your little sister. That's f***ed up."

With glazed, red swollen eyes, Franni's son responded, "Beyond f***ed up. F***ing cancer, dude. I can't even begin to describe the pain. F**k life. There is nothin' to live for. F**k it, no meaning, no purpose. Maybe I'll smoke weed and drink whiskey until I f***ing die." About that time, a police car rolled up behind them. Franni's son was first to notice. "S**t !"

One of the kids in the back, with great panic, asked, "What the hell are we gonna do?" The grief-stricken driver didn't say a word. He adjusted himself properly in the seat, started the engine, put it in drive, grabbed the steering wheel with a steely look of determination, and then punched the gas.

In unison, the two other boys started screaming, "What the hell are you. Stop— don't— doing? We can't—oh s**t! This s**t will make it f***ing worse!" Franni's son was oblivious to their words. The high speed chase was on. The boy weaved his way around other cars with reckless abandon.

Snake howled with excitement and laughter. "In exactly six minutes and sixty six seconds—wham! The boy will be in hell!"

Francesca cried out, "No, son!"

Magnus's first instinct was to punch the invisible wall. He was crazed with hatred toward Snake. However, the lessons from his praying grandmother came to his mind. He calmly went to his knees. Twenty seconds later, he arose. He calmly stepped through the plasma-like invisible wall. Snake was so giddy with pleasure, he didn't notice. Molech tugged at his master's sleeve. "What is it?" Molech didn't utter a word. He simply pointed toward Magnus.

Snake tried to hide his concern, and said, "Well, well, well."

Now three other police cars joined the chase. The boy was headed toward the freeway. He was going to put the pedal to the medal. At times, he had to drive on the sidewalk. Since it

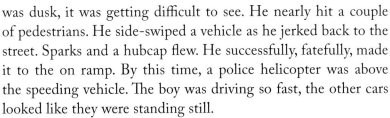

was dusk, it was getting difficult to see. He nearly hit a couple of pedestrians. He side-swiped a vehicle as he jerked back to the street. Sparks and a hubcap flew. He successfully, fatefully, made it to the on ramp. By this time, a police helicopter was above the speeding vehicle. The boy was driving so fast, the other cars looked like they were standing still.

Magnus remembered Robert's act of ultimate heroism. While he thought about Andrea and Dawn, he knew he had to fight against evil, not only for humanity, but for his sister as well. Magnus went to one knee in prayer, came up slowly, took a deep breath, and began the sprint toward the evil one. Snake thought, *Surely he has an inkling of fear and respect for me. He won't go through with this. I'm S-s-snake!*

As Magnus was about to dive into the middle of the prince of darkness, he was tackled from the side. It was Will Vanderburgh. Snake, Magnus, and especially Will were shocked that he did that. After Magnus quickly collected his wits, he questioned, "Will, what are you doing? By the way, where is your t-shirt from?"

"Uh, Devil's Tower Monument in Wyoming."

"Fitting."

Guffawing, Snake responded, "Fitting! T-shirt! Fitting! T-shirt! Magnus, where in hades did you get your jocularity!" Not only did Snake genuinely find the response funny, but he was pleased with the continued delay of whatever action Magnus was contemplating.

After a few of seconds, when Magnus and Will finished their blank stare at Snake, Will continued, "Anyway, I caused this mess. You have a family, I don't. I'll do this. I convinced the director to let me go. I preset the calculations—I believe with ninety-five percent certainty—so that you and Francesca can get back."

There was now a little less than a minute until the crash. Would it really be the end of Francesca's future son, the end of her sanity? Would it be the end of Magnus's hope and strength? Magnus argued with Will, "You might have a family someday. You're still young." Snake was pleased with the discussion between the two agents. It distracted them. There were only seconds left.

It was the tail end of the rush hour traffic. There were many cars, but they were flowing at a descent pace. The young man jerked the car to the right, onto the shoulder. He accelerated. It was too late to see the stalled semi on the same shoulder just ahead.

Snake was satisfied. He knew Will didn't have it in him. In fact, Will was too scared as he faced the imposing figure. He looked at Magnus then Francesca and for a split second, from somewhere deep within, Vanderburgh did muster enough courage. Maybe the brief moment of levity helped. He sprinted toward the demon.

The passengers screamed when they realized they were going to slam into the back-end of the semi-truck. Francesca's son hit the brakes. The car skidded. It was too late, though.

Will dove. As he entered the mid-section of Snake, all the holograms shattered. All that was left were Franni and Magnus, lying on the ground at the edge of the Gray Cliff. Nothing was around them except gray sky, gray rock, gray dust, and the edge of the abyss.

Magnus helped Francesca to her feet. She was scared, shaken, but okay. Magnus wasn't slow to lead. He said, "We need to find a tunnel and follow the light. There should be signs, people and things from our past maybe, pointing us in the right direction. We need to get to the portal: round, eight-by-eight foot, pulsates light. That's how we get back home. Let's go."

After a couple of minutes of walking, Franni spoke, "You certainly know a lot about this realm."

"Yeah, I wish I didn't. Of course, I'm sure there are many things I don't know. I probably only comprehend the tip of the iceberg, if that much."

Francesca was amazed at Magnus's knowledge. It was just as he said: They found the tunnel, followed the ever-present source

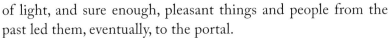

of light, and sure enough, pleasant things and people from the past led them, eventually, to the portal.

When they returned, Rick was restrained. He looked and sounded crazy. He mumbled and laughed to himself. There was also a gurney with a sheet covered body on it. Magnus knew it was Will. In all, there was the director, five agents, and one coroner when they returned. The director told Magnus, "Take a few days off. Rest. I'll see you at 0800 hours Monday morning for a debriefing."

———

The following evening, the entire family, except for Dawn who was asleep in her crib, sat and relaxed in the living room. Everyone noticed that Magnus, though fatigued, was a different man in a good way. Dorcus began the conversation, "I'm so interested in your CIA work. I wish I could understand more of what it is you actually do."

"Yeah, Grandma, I wish I could understand exactly what I do also."

Francesca chimed in, "It's pretty cool stuff I think."

It was a little awkward. Each person in the room didn't know exactly who knew what. After a period of silence, Francesca broke the mood. She looked at her grandmother and said, "I think it's time." Dorcus agreed.

Magnus asked, "Time for what?"

Dorcus replied, "Time for you to get some rest, my dear boy."

Magnus responded, "I could use some shut-eye. I'm tired."

Magnus kissed his grandmother on the cheek, his sister on the forehead, and his wife on the lips, and said, "Good night."

Magnus vaguely remembered his head touching the pillow. In the middle of the night he barely awoke in time to see a shadowy figure standing over him. Before he could react, he was tranquilized. He had no idea who it was. It was too dark in the room for him to see it was his sweet, little sister!

CHAPTER 33

BIGGER MISSION

Magnus awoke on a comfortable, rustic couch. It was in a warm, cozy log cabin. It smelled fresh. Though groggy, Magnus got himself into a seated position. There was a nice, low fire going and sitting around a table were Dorcus, Francesca, and Stan Johnston. Stan was a middle aged man who was the Assistant Directorate of Science and Technology at the CIA. Magnus was perplexed, *What the—why am I here? Why is Johnston here?*

At the table, besides wonderful smelling coffee, there was a conference phone. On the closest wall, there was a suspended flat screen TV. The dining area was set for a meeting. Magnus was the first to speak as he stood up to look out the window. All he saw was pine trees. There was no body of water, no hills, and no mountains. "Mr. Johnston, where is your drab, gray suit, cheap short sleeve dress shirt, and clip on tie? Oh, and those out of style wire frame glasses?"

Dorcus corrected Magnus, "Be polite."

"Well, Grandma, please forgive me for being a little irritable, but I was obviously tranquilized and brought to Grizzly Adam's condo against my will! I just finished a taxing mission! I am a little grumpy! By the way, why are you and Franni here?"

Mr. Johnston chimed in, "It's okay, Dorcus. I think I can empathize somewhat with how he feels. I was brought to the Demonic Terrorism Department in similar fashion."

Turning to Magnus, he said, "That clashing wardrobe you just described is my undercover. This hipper Land's End look is more me." Francesca rolled her eyes.

Francesca brought Magnus a cup of coffee just the way he likes, with a small shot of flavored creamer and about a tea spoon

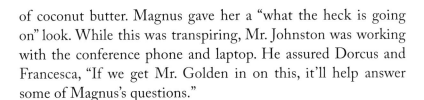

of coconut butter. Magnus gave her a "what the heck is going on" look. While this was transpiring, Mr. Johnston was working with the conference phone and laptop. He assured Dorcus and Francesca, "If we get Mr. Golden in on this, it'll help answer some of Magnus's questions."

No sooner said then an older, very distinguished gentleman appeared on the screen. The man said, "Hello, team, and welcome Mr. Stone. It's an honor to have you here."

Magnus didn't hesitate, "Why am I here?"

"Your insight into the spiritual realm could be the breakthrough I've been hoping for since I started my research over twenty-five years ago. You see—may I call you Magnus?"

"No you may not."

Not at all vexed, Mr. Golden continued, "Mr. Stone, I've been studying and exploring the demonic world for all these years. So far, it's been through archeological exploration, books, and the Internet. But now, now I've found someone whose encountered demons face to face, multiple times."

Dorcus weighed in, "You see, my son, you fight evil in the physical world, which is very important. However, there are spiritual forces at work behind these wicked people. You understand those forces probably better than anyone now."

"And why are you here, Grandma?"

"It's in our Stone blood. I'm sort of a spy too."

"Sort of?"

Dorcus continued, "You know how deeply I study the Bible. Not as much since my eyesight failed, but I'm still able to maintain my love of the Scripture through audio. You know I constantly listen to the news, and of course, I offer constant vigilant prayer support for this important work."

Magnus, still miffed, questioned, "What is this work?"

Mr. Golden resumed, "This work—and by the way, your humble grandmother is a tremendous asset with her insight and wisdom—this work is fighting evil from the inside of man."

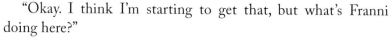

"Okay. I think I'm starting to get that, but what's Franni doing here?"

Mr. Golden answered, "She's a very valuable part of this team as well. She's a young woman of character, strength, and virtue, I don't have to tell you that, and she believes. I'll stop now and let Francesca explain herself. She can do it far better than I."

Francesca got comfortable and started, "Our wonderful grandmother has taught us much. She's passed on to me the love of God and the hatred of evil. I do believe in the demonic realm, and thanks to you, I believe now more than ever. I saw how it drove Rick Munson—"

Magnus interjected, "How did he lure you to the lab? Wait, maybe I don't want to know?"

"Well, he didn't exactly lure me. I seduced him. From the inside of the CIA, Mr. Johnston knew, or at least had a strong hunch, what Will and Rick were up to. I flirted with Munson. We figured somehow he would try to use me to get to you. He would be my 'in,' so to speak."

Magnus, now visibly more perturbed, questioned Mr. Johnston, "Hold on, you spied within the Agency, you leaked classified information outside the Agency, and you endangered my sister?"

Mr. Johnston tried to speak, "I—"

"You breeched security and put my sister at risk?!"

Dorcus, in her even, calm voice said, "Magnus, please." Magnus jumped up and stormed around the room. The four gave him some space and time.

Mr. Johnston resumed, "I was extremely apprehensive about planting Francesca like that, as was Dorcus and Mr. Golden. Your sister insisted it was the best and possibly the only way to get so close to Munson. Fortunately, it worked. It was a risk, one we didn't take lightly."

Mr. Golden added, "Mr. Stone, the unseen, demonic realm has perpetrated incredible misery, through human agents, in the world for a long time. We wrestle against principalities and powers

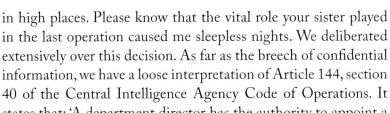

in high places. Please know that the vital role your sister played in the last operation caused me sleepless nights. We deliberated extensively over this decision. As far as the breech of confidential information, we have a loose interpretation of Article 144, section 40 of the Central Intelligence Agency Code of Operations. It states that: 'A department director has the authority to appoint a subcommittee as needed.' so you see, we are a 'subcommittee.' The Unconventional Terrorism Department is a level deeper than the CIA counter terrorism strand. Our subcommittee is called the Demonic Terrorism Department. It is a level even deeper."

Magnus broke in, "I'm sure that article doesn't mean appointing someone from the outside, like you, my grandmother, and my sister, but I suppose that's where the 'loose interpretation' comes into play. Let me guess, your one of the heirs of the Golden family, as in Golden Aviation, needless to say this DTD is well funded."

"Correct, young man."

Dorcus spoke, "Mr. Golden, Mr. Johnston, may Francesca, Magnus, and I go outside for some fresh air? We've laid a lot on my grandson. I think the outdoors and time alone with Franni and I will help."

Mr. Golden and Mr. Johnston nodded their approval. "Absolutely," said Mr. Golden. "The fresh air is a godsend."

Francesca suggested, "There is a stream not too far down the road. It has a bench right by it also. I think that would be the ideal place for us to sit for a while." Magnus helped his grandmother put on her sweater, Francesca and Magnus put on their jackets, and then the three exited.

It was a moving sight: The three of them walking slowly down the road. Magnus was on Dorcus' right and Francesca on her left. Dorcus was holding the arms of her beloved grandchildren. When they arrived at the spot, it was a little more cloudy than sunny. However, with the right outerwear, it felt good. The sound of the stream was relaxing. They sat in quiet for a few minutes. Magnus broke the silence, "I don't want you two involved in anything dangerous."

Francesca really wanted to respond, however, she waited for her grandmother to speak. Francesca was becoming a woman of discretion. After a thoughtful pause, Dorcus said, "I'm at the end of my life. What could happen to me? Besides, I really feel like I have a strong sense of purpose being a part of the DTD. You know better than any of us how real demons are, how they motivate people. I only have somewhat of a grasp on it through the Bible, life experience, and the news. It's sickening what evil will cause people to do: Walk into a school and shoot innocent young people in cold blood, detonate a bomb with no regard for the innocent people who might be at the wrong place at the wrong time, and drive people to hurt and kill babies and children. I guess that's, ultimately, why I'm lending my support: the babies and children. Now, having said that, I do understand the concern for your tenacious sister, but again, I believe this is a much greater eternal purpose. This life we live, an average of seventy or eighty years, is a snap of the finger compared to eternity; I believe what Franni is endeavoring to do is noble. Yes, I worry and pray for her constantly. Ultimately, His will be done."

It was Francesca's turn. "Being so close to evil, which was terrifying, strengthened my resolve that this mission—the Demonic Terrorism Department—is vital. I want to be a part of something good and important."

Magnus said, "Staying safe, being a good wife and mother—those are very good and very important too. You're so young; you have your whole life ahead of you."

Francesca quickly came back with, "Look at you. You're a wonderful family man and a spy."

"You're tough to argue with, lil' sis."

"Then don't."

After putting Francesca in a gentle headlock and giving her a gentle noogie, he said, "Let's go back to the cabin. I have a few more questions for Mr. Golden and Mr. Johnston."

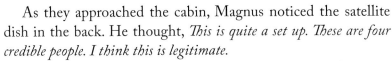

As they approached the cabin, Magnus noticed the satellite dish in the back. He thought, *This is quite a set up. These are four credible people. I think this is legitimate.*

When the three walked into the cabin, there was a split screen on the monitor. Mr. Golden was on the left half. On the right was a shadowy figure. He was unrecognizable by design.

Mr. Johnston said to Magnus, "Allow me to introduce to you, Mr. A. Z."

Magnus said, "As in Alpha and Omega?"

An electronically garbled voice said, "Well done, young man, you know some Greek. Mr. Golden and Mr. Johnston said you have some concerns about the authority of the DTD. I respect and understand that. I authorized it. I'm a high ranking official in the Administrative Branch of the Federal Government. I choose to remain unknown to everyone except Mr. Golden; I do this for political reasons. This whole misnomer of 'the separation of church and state' is nonsense. The first time the phrase appeared was in a letter by Thomas Jefferson to a Christian group. The purpose was to keep the government out of the affairs of the church, not the other way around, but the hedonistic, secular humanistic religious disciples high jacked the phrase and distorted, manipulated, and twisted it into what it is today. Sorry, that's a sore subject with me. I didn't mean to get started. Anyway, I believe strongly in the demonic realm. Fighting evil at its root cause is vital. That's what the Demonic Terrorism Department does. You can't explain this to a room full of legislators. Mr. Stone, please join us. We need you. I would be thrilled and honored to have you as a part of this team. We meet here once a month and AD hoc when the need arises. I'll leave you to ponder, Joshua. Regardless of what you decide, thank you for all of your tremendous service to this country." Mr. A. Z.'s side of the screen went blank, the room was silent, and Magnus was deep in thought.

After thirty seconds of anticipation of what Magnus would say and do, he said, jokingly, but without a smile, "I'm tired of being sedated. I'm in."

CHAPTER 34

THE VOW

B ack in the massive throne room of evil, Baal's throne would remain unoccupied forever. However, Snake's would not. Molech, seizing what he thought was opportunity, decided to assert as the new leader. He thought, *It's my time. I've waited four thousand years.*

He stated to the Elders of Evil, "It's my chronology." He confidently strode up to the big throne then proceeded to presumptuously make himself comfortable in it. He spoke to himself, yet loud enough for the rest of the elders to hear, "Yes, it is comely."

From the back of the great cavern a weak shuffle could be heard. It got louder and louder. Finally, the elders were able to recognize the bent over, strengthless figure of Snake approaching the cave and hall throne. He was wheezing. He had to stop periodically to catch his breath. It should have taken only seconds to reach the throne, but it took him minutes because of his weak state.

The elders watched him as he struggled to the foot of the great throne where Molech proudly sat. He paused to catch his breath. Then, he took a deep breath, let out a vicious growl, and charged Molech. He backhanded him so hard, Molech flew through the air and crashed into the wall on the side, about a quarter of a mile away. Yes, Snake was truly a shell of his former self. In his prime, he would have knocked him through the wall.

Snake then collapsed into his throne totally exhausted. In almost the exact way Snake approached his throne a few moments earlier, Molech approached his smaller seat among the elders. He too, collapsed into it when he finally got there. After regaining some semblance of strength, Snake crashed his fist into the arm of his throne and said, "We've lost this battle, but the war is not over. We will continue the fight of evil over good!"